The Catterthorough Peak Embassy

Volume 1: The Battle For Beige

This book is for Dad, who liked cats and books, and who would have been interested; and for First Employee, who downloaded whatever programme it is I'm using and forced me to finish and upload the kindle version of this; because if anyone can see a Strategic Plan through to a conclusion it's him.

Contents

Preface	4
Chapter 1: Introductions	5
Chapter 2: What passes for Summer 2021 in the High Peak	9
Chapter 3: Autumn 2021, when we Hunker Down	16
Chapter 4: Winter 21/22: The Polar Night Approaches	53
Chapter 5: Spring 2022 is sprung, the grass is riz, and we all know where the birdies is	90
Chapter 6: Summer 2022: Sausage Rolls and Demonic Cakes	139
Chapter 7: Autumn 2022: Second Employee begins her long and interesting career of telling people to shove their JOBS right up their BUMS	176
Chapter 8: December 2022: the fight to keep Christmas Aesthetic	214

Preface

Thank you to all the lovely people on the Larry The Downing Street Cat For Prime Minister! facebook group, who have been so kind to Ghost and Esso: and who are all much funnier than me. An excellent bunch of Cats and Employees, and I'm glad I found you all x

Chapter 1

Introductions

Well. Well. It's very much a point of pride to me that our - my and my sister, Ghost's - carefully, professionally written Briefing Notes and Updates to Larry, have become such a source of Moral Guidance to the Nation in latter years and through these difficult, confusing times that we've been asked to collate them into a volume for easier perusal by Clumsy Ape-Descended Employees!

Call me a dreamer (although I'm not the only one), but I like to think that having this collection available will contribute, in some small way, to developing a Greater Backbone throughout the nation: to the rebuilding of community: perhaps to improving the inadequate toilet rolls now sold by Waitrose, or even to reinvigorating the post-industrial Midlands. That is my dream. I hope you, the reader, benefit from these Notes and don't find them too Serious and Intellectual - if you do, you must persevere! Remember, at all times, how my dedication to Strategic Plan Delivery has improved everyone and everything around me, and be inspired thereby to Do Better yourself!

Esso, Ambassador to the High Peak

Oh for Bast's sake, Esso, I said we're explaining what's going on in case there's ever anyone reading this book who isn't either related to or friends with Second Employee, not being pompous or going off on our own Hobby Horses (however right we might be about Waitrose Toilet Roll Inadequacy). Anyway. I'll do it myself AS EVER.

Hello everyone. I'm Ghost, and my brother Esso and I have held the Extremely Important Roles of Joint Feline Ambassadors to

the High Peak since 2019. It's probably THE most important role in the Feline Diplomatic Service, and we try very hard to bring Gracious Living and Efficient Delivery of the High Peak Embassy Strategic Plan to Buxton, where the Embassy is based. We started making our Briefing Notes and Updates To Prime Minister Larry the Cat available to the wider Catinet (the Parliamentary Cabinet Of Cats, for those Employees reading this who are Very Obtuse) once we were properly settled into the job, and I *personally* like to think it's been helpful and instructive for everyone. Esso, for reasons known only to himself, made one of our Employees Official Archivist, and she has very carefully copied down our Updates and other Clevernesses in her best handwriting and got it into a form that people can download to their Kindles, which has been a process which has taken a really unprecedented amount of Coffee, Cake, and Confusion!

But I really think publishing our Collected Updates is absolutely vital for everyone to appreciate Quite How Difficult it is to try to enforce efficiency when one is living in a Very Tall Embassy with Particularly Incapable Employees and trying to ward off the forces of chaos with the moral equivalent of a small wooden fork and a toothpick. That is how it feels. And I hope everyone reading this is impressed by my efforts in what really are almost impossible circumstances. But I would not like to leave you on a depressing note. Read and be inspired! (That's an instruction, not a suggestion, and I *will* be checking afterwards).

Ghost, also Ambassador to the High Peak (you may at the end of this book consider me to be the more dynamic one. I couldn't possibly comment at this stage)

Chapter 2

What passes for Summer 2021 in the High Peak

August 2021

Larry and the Catinet: my name is Esso and I'd like to introduce myself properly. You've probably seen my name come up repeatedly in Ministerial Papers: but I thought it might just be helpful to do a more formal introduction. I and my sister Ghost (she's black and white, just like me, but it's distributed very, very slightly differently: e.g., I have thirty white hairs just underneath my chin, whereas Ghost has probably about three million, all over her body, with the addition of Three Discrete Black Patches, a Black Tail, and a Black Smudge On Her Nosie. It's just a different look. It doesn't make her any more stylish than me. Lots of people have admired my Coat Of Almost Uninterrupted Velvety Midnight) are Feline Ambassadors to the High Peak.

We were deployed here a couple of years ago, from a short-lived temporary role in Sue at Cats' Protection's Garage, where our Strategic Potential was immediately recognised. We were allocated an Embassy, and we immediately appointed two employees, First Employee and Second Employee, although Ghost does say, if there'd been a wider field of applicants, she *personally* might have made different decisions. For my part, Larry, I really think we've done an excellent job since we arrived! There's been a lot of diplomatic work to do establishing borders (particularly with Grey Next Door Cat), and I've absolutely been flat out: but Ghost says she thinks the High Peak is an awful, cold place where it even snows in May; and if it hadn't been for me and my 'boring colour that nobody wants' she could have had her pick of other Embassies.

Sometimes when it's been raining a lot she says to me, look what beautiful markings I have on my fur, Esso: you were literally the only thing standing between me and a lovely cottage in the Derbyshire Dales with Dreamies on tap where at least they would have had more than two weeks of summer.

That makes me very sad; because I really do put my heart into our work here, and it's taken me so long to get our employees anywhere near up to scratch (I don't like to tell them this and demotivate them, but they were a bit useless to start with, particularly Second Employee, bless her). Anyway it's nice to make your and the Catinet's acquaintance formally. I have to go now, I have to begin my evening diplomatic duties of standing on the wall outside and peering at Viv next door through her window with a disturbing intensity. Mine isn't an easy calling; but I really think it's worthwhile.

August 2021

Dear Larry and the Catinet.

Hello everyone. My name is Ghost, and I'm joint Feline Ambassador to the High Peak with my brother, Esso. Esso tells me he said hello to everyone yesterday, so I thought I'd better just *nip along* to correct all the misapprehensions he'll have left you with. Esso and I look almost identical, but, if you look very, very carefully, it's possible to see that I have slightly finer features - there's also a tiny difference in how the black and white is distributed in our fur, but I know it takes a very highly trained eye to spot that. Don't worry if when you meet me you miss it.

Anyway, I suspect Esso might have given you the impression yesterday that I've done nothing but moan since we were sent to be Ambassadors at this appalling cold outpost where all the pavements are covered in sheet ice for six months of the year and everywhere is uphill in both directions. Well, that isn't true! I've been very good about accepting my fate. As the nice lady at Cats' Protection said to me, during one of our little chats while Esso and I were waiting to be allocated our first Embassy: look, Ghostycat, what with Esso's little biting problem and black cats being a real bugger to rehome, you'll basically just have to have the first suckers who look as if they won't make you both straight into hats, and try to make the best of it. And so I have! Esso said not to tell you about the little biting problem, and especially not about the time he bit Second Employee's Father and caused an international (England/Cornwall) diplomatic incident and a Covid scare. So I haven't. I'll also let him carry on pretending it was him who established the border agreement with Grey Next Door Cat, even though it was me and it took a lot of negotiating!

Anyway have a nice evening. I'm off to sit under the sofa so I can grab Second Employee's ankle the minute she's forgotten I'm there. It's a lovely daily bonding experience for both of us, and I know how much she enjoys it by the way she squeals.

August 2021

Hello Larry and the rest of the Catinet! It's Ghost here again, Joint Ambassador to the High Peak. Right. Let me set the scene for you: the High Peak is an extremely cultured place. The town we live in has an Opera Festival, a Gilbert and Sullivan Festival, and a Fringe Festival; in fact you can barely walk to Waitrose in July without starting a Festival by mistake. It is a very real danger. I really have to keep an eye on Second Employee in that regard, because honestly that's the last thing I need, coming home after an extensive diplomatic mission to find a lot of people dressed in Seasalt organic linen sitting on Our Back Steps expecting a witty new interpretation of madrigals.

Anyway, an extremely important part of my role is being right at the forefront of Appreciating Art and Culture. This week, for example, has been spent critically evaluating a painting Second Employee has found randomly at the back of a cupboard. It really is rather difficult to describe: but basically it is a portrait of something which purports to be a Cherub, but in reality looks like Sid James with a moustache and a hangover. Apparently she painted it at an evening class a long time ago 'when I lived a very long way away, without any Festivals or judgemental cats like you, Ghost'. Because of my very highly-developed sense of artistic taste, I was able to tell her that it is terrible, and should go straight back into the cupboard. I mean, I don't really expect any better from the large apes, but goodness me.

The Employees have always been a bit challenging in this respect: forever finding dodgy pictures from somewhere, and a very cavalier approach to Embassy Decor. As I say to Second Employee in our daily appraisal (her)/ stroking (me) sessions, try getting rid of some of your artist friends and making a few instead who're good at gardening, then Esso and I won't have to keep going next door to sit in theirs, and I'm sure you'd enjoy being able to grow something a bit more exciting than mint and a few droopy petunias.

Esso says he doesn't mind too much about the pictures and the petunias because he's very focussed on being a Cultural Ambassador with a special interest in music; but all he means

IN REALITY is that he enjoys sitting on the piano stool because it gets all the sun in the evenings. I'm afraid Esso still has quite a way to go before he's in any danger of reaching my artistic heights!

August 2021

Hello Larry and the Catinet.

This is Esso here, Ambassador to the High Peak. Well, there have been unwelcome developments. Second Employee confessed yesterday that she's abandoning us for three weeks. We are furious! A temporary employee has been allocated - Interim Summer Employee - but we're still unhappy. I trapped her on the sofa for two hours yesterday to stop her packing, and Ghost has followed her everywhere ever since with her special poignant expression. I've never seen a cat with a more poignant expression, so it's been very effective. We're fairly sure we've broken her emotionally, but she may still manage to escape. We'll keep you appraised of the situation.

Second Employee has tried to explain herself: it turns out that, when she married First Employee and he came back from living A Life Of Shallow Depravity on the Costa Del Sol to settle with her in Derbyshire where there is very little Depravity and basically no Sol at all, she had to agree they would go back occasionally so he could remind himself what it was like to eat

Espetos on the Beach, which apparently isn't easy to do here, even if you go as far as Chapel En Le Frith. Well, I really find that hard to believe. She said it was 'basically like having eaten the pomegranate seeds' and 'you know I don't like going on holiday, Esso, don't make me feel worse than I do already'. Well! That is all I can say. Well! And I have suggested to Second Employee that she makes sure to declare this Type Of Thing on the application form for all future diplomatic support positions!

Chapter 3

Autumn 2021, when we Hunker Down

September 2021

Larry and the Catinet, it's Ghost here, Joint Ambassador to the High Peak, with my Informative Update. I'm letting you know that our employees are FINALLY back after being away for three weeks. Three weeks! I'm surprised Second Employee *in particular* could manage to count to three and get the right ferry back. We suffered dreadfully, of course. They arranged for Interim Summer Employee to come and live with us 'because he's nice, Ghost, you'll like him, and he's good with cats'. Well, yes, he was excellent: he was much better than them: but the point is, it's a dereliction of duty, and that makes any Ambassador discombobulated. Esso said so long as he had his dinner and a functioning cat flap he was happy; but I kept thinking, where are they now. Are they, for example, sitting staring at the sea, thinking, how long until we see Ghostycat again.

[Note from Esso: I suspect this is absolutely what Second Employee does all the time she is away, rather than doing Improving Things like going to Museums or attempting her Duolingo Spanish.]

Esso says I pined, but of course I didn't; although I suppose I stared a little bit sadly at Interim Summer Employee, or at least I suppose it could have been interpreted that way; and I lay droopily on Second Employee's dressing gown that she's left for me, looking poignant. Anyway then I decided briskly that Enough Was Enough, and I had a really good idea: Esso and I sacrificed a couple of mice on their bed to bring them back. And it worked. So I shall do that again when necessary, and I recommend it to all other Feline Employers. It's not that I care about our employees, you understand; it's just that they're *my responsibility*, and they need to be *here* and not wandering round Andalucia causing trouble. I shall be having strict words and reminding them they've used up their annual leave entitlement for the next ten years after this!

September 2021

Larry and the Catinet, Esso here, Ambassador to the High Peak. Well, it's winter here now - it might start to get warm again around June 2022 - so part of my and Ghost's role as Ambassadors is to be very robust about the slightly challenging weather, and set an example to the natives. That's why I noted in shocked disapproval earlier Ghosty making herself a veritable cocoon out of a throw on the sofa and hiding from the drizzle. Nesh, I think they call it up here! You'll be pleased to hear I managed to get her out for a healthy jog around the garden later! We can't have weakness in the Embassy!

September 2021

Larry and the Catinet, this is Ghost here, Ambassador to the High Peak. I'm notifying you that I had to do a Special Judgy Expression earlier. I shall set the scene. I was relaxing on the rug in the sitting room, when Second Employee wandered in with a Large Silly Vase full of Gladioli. It was enormous. It had stripes in a Particularly Unfortunate Brown, and Orange. Where would she have *found* such a thing? Why would she have decided to drag it back to the Embassy? Was it purchased in a Sensible Shop? I really do not think it was. I have therefore instructed Second Employee to have a good tidy up and declutter; she's muttering about the vase being genuine West German 1970s Ceramics and wanting to keep it, but I'm ignoring her. I wouldn't have mosaiced the fireplace surround either, like she did before Esso and I arrived here to supervise appropriately; but Second Employee just won't be said, no matter how many times I've said to her, look, just paint this entire house all over in Farrow and Ball Ammonite or more realistically in one of its many cheaper imitations, and we'll call it a day. She'd like you to know also that she knows the gladioli are bad for cats, and she watches me so I don't eat them. Hmmm, Second Employee, that's what you think.

September 2021

Hello Larry, and the Catinet, this is Esso, Ambassador to the High Peak checking in. I'd like you all to know that I take my responsibilities as an employer very seriously; as you'll all remember, I was really rather a star at the last Feline HR Update Teams Session; and today I sat on Second Employee for hours, as per the High Peak Embassy Strategic Plan 2021-2022 Appendix J3 Occupational Health Policy (final). I had to chase her down three floors, biting her toes, but I got her pinned down on that sofa in the end. She kept saying, look Esso, I've got to move you on now, I want to get to Aldi because we've run out of milk. But I didn't listen, because our employees drink far too much coffee anyway, and besides, I know what she's like, 'just popping out for milk'' and sneaking back later with three cheese plants, a waffle maker, and a box of Tunnocks Teacakes. Much better to sit quietly and stroke my lovely velvety fur. Practice your mindfulness, Second Employee!

September 2021

Larry and the Catinet, Esso here, Ambassador to the High Peak. I worked unusually hard today and gave Second Employee her appraisal. I curled up on her lap, rested my eyes and put my paw over my NOSIE while she thought about how well she was really doing against her Key Performance Indicators (i.e., not very): I find Paws On Nosies promotes honesty in Employees. Ghost is annoyed with me. She says she's the one who appraises Second Employee, and I can, and I quote, 'sling my hook', because apparently Second Employee has been moaning that she can't get anything done because she's always got a cat attached to her; but Ghost says, who else is she going to do her kneading on, so she can't have me 'using up all of Second Employee's energy and goodwill'. I did suggest to Ghost that she could go and knead on First Employee instead, but she gave me what I believe is called an old-fashioned look. We both understood. Second Employee will just have to deal with it, I'm afraid.

September 2021

Larry and the Catinet: it's Ghost and Esso here, joint Ambassadors to the High Peak. We're just checking in to let you know how busy we are and how constructive we're being. We're keeping a close eye on things up here. We've had a good look under the Sitting Room Rug, it turned out not to be suspicious but we're glad we checked, so we checked a few more times by making it into a tunnel and skidding into it at speed. Now we're doing our Intense Joint Stare at Second Employee; we think it's very unlikely she's going to do anything interesting based on our past experience, but if she does, we're right here on the spot. We hope the Catinet is impressed by our vigilance. P.s. Ghost says she's such an excellent Ambassador, it wouldn't kill the Catinet to redeploy her somewhere 'a bit bloody warmer and with a few less bloody hills', so we're just putting that one out there.

September 2021

Larry and the Catinet, this is Esso, Ambassador to the High Peak reporting again. I had a very thought-provoking experience yesterday, which made me ponder the nature of our relationship with the Employees. It was early evening: the sun had just set: I was out on patrol around the street behind our house. I'd just been down to check on the heron who lives near the river, and I was popping back home via a good hard stare at the white cat down the road (he's a bold one, he is) when I saw First and Second Employee 'having a walk into town'. Well! I'd left Second Employee on her bum on the sofa, as usual, and I'd promised Ghost I wouldn't let her out of my sight, because the last time we lost control of the situation Second Employee went away for three weeks and understandably, Ghost was worried. She asked me every single day, is Second Employee coming back today, and honestly I can't go through that again. So this time I was cunning and proactive. I strode right up to Second Employee and said, look you, what are you doing wandering about in the dark without a by your leave, I'm taking you back home. 'Oh God!' she said. 'Esso, you frightened me to death, lurking in the dark and squeaking at me'. Then she said to First Employee, 'look, it's Esso! I'd better walk back with him or he'll follow us right into town. You carry on to your meeting, I was only coming for the walk'.

Well, I gave Second Employee a fair old piece of my mind as we walked back together. Look, Second Employee, I said, if you'd seen Ghost moping about when you weren't here for those three weeks you wouldn't be playing fast and loose like this. I got her back in, settled her on the sofa with her laptop and a cup of tea, and then I popped out again to resume hostilities with White Cat. Ghost told me a funny thing later though. Ghost said, when First Employee came back, Second Employee said to him, do you know, I had a strange thought after I texted you to say I'd got Esso home safe after we found him wandering about. What if he actually thought he'd got me home safe after he'd found me wandering about?! And then they both looked at each other thoughtfully and sat in silence for a bit. That's an insight into the funny way their minds work, isn't it? They're quite dim creatures, but we have to be patient and kind, because their brains are very small, and they can't help it.

September 2021

Larry and the Catinet, this is Ghost, Ambassador to the High Peak, with something *extremely* disappointing to report. Well, you won't believe this, because Esso and I didn't; but apparently Second Employee has been moonlighting! Yes! She thinks she's got another job! Today she sat and did something called a 'bank reconciliation', which you do by flapping lots of bits of paper about, eating chocolate munch munch munch, and swearing. It meant that Esso and I couldn't knead her or sit on her, and we were very discombobulated; because I have been *absolutely clear* to Second Employee that the main bullet point in her job description - indeed, the only bullet point - is being available for kneading and sitting and stroking at all times, like a mildly animated cushion. So Esso sat and stared at her and I made my feelings known vocally with my special Shrill Squeak. Sort it out, Second Employee!

Esso says we have to be kind, because Second Employee came from a bad situation, and is our rescue animal. But I say, it's time to get over that now, and Second Employee needs to get some proper stroking done tomorrow and to tell me again about how I've got the softest fur in Buxton!

September 2021

Larry and the Catinet; in my update today you will see a Dramatic Exposition of Diplomacy In Difficult Circumstances, which I think you will find Enormously Instructive: so you will want to pay close attention.

As you can imagine, a very large part of my Ambassadorial Role is cementing diplomatic relations: and, today, Second

Employee's parents 'called round for a quick coffee', and Ghost and I were able to *really put some work* into building bridges with Second Employee's mother. Second Employee's mother is a woman who once *rather* overreacted to an unfortunate and completely random incident that happened a very long time ago which anyone normal would have completely forgotten by now and not borne a grudge about. However, she *has* borne a grudge; and ever since, whenever she sees us, she is Nervous.

At the time of the Unimportant Random Incident, our employees had gone to stay in A Mousehole in Cornwall without taking us (selfishly); and Second Employee's parents were providing Interim Cover. It just so happened one day that, very unfortunately, Second Employee's father *somehow* managed to become bitten by my teeth; which incident of course was nobody's fault, and especially not mine. It was also not my fault that he managed *somehow* to get an infection from the bite that may or may not have happened and also no causal connection was ever proved; and it was *definitely* not my fault that then, because he had a temperature, he had to be quarantined with Second Employee's mother - and us - until he got a negative Covid test; which, because it was last year and everyone was only just out of lockdown, admittedly took a surprisingly long time. Anyway, Ghost and I discussed the situation afterwards, and decided it was actually a really good thing that Second Employee's mother had rung up Second Employee to tell her she was 'trapped in this silly mad house with your father and two mad cats which might *attack me at any moment!*' and made them both come back early from their Mousehole: because, Ghost had had no-one to knead on for nearly a week, and it was, frankly, getting a bit much. So it turned out well for us.

I didn't, of course, offer that interpretation to Second Employee's mother today; because I'm not completely sure she's quite ready to listen to Sensible Views, given that she mostly peered at me from behind doors, saying, is that cat going to bite people again. I found that rather hurtful. But then I rallied: I thought of my diplomacy training, and so I lay on the sofa all the time they were here, looking velvety and adorable and as if butter wouldn't melt in my gentle mouth which has gentle teeth in it; and after a while Second Employee's mother was almost able to sit in the same room as me, that's how successful I was.

I really consider today a triumph of my diplomatic skills. In fact, if I think about the whole affair in the proper light, the only ones actually to blame were the Employees. Imagine going to A Mousehole and not bringing me back a mouse!

October 2021

Larry and the Catinet: Ghost here, Ambassador to the High Peak, updating on diplomatic progress.

Larry! I am so annoyed with Esso today! Second Employee was making dinner, and frankly she was making quite heavy weather of it: because First Employee had made her go swimming in the Outdoor Pool, and whenever Second Employee does any exercise at all she thinks she should spend the rest of the day lying on her back on the sofa and only lifting her head up to eat cake. Anyway, Esso said it was high time we began Phase Two of the High Peak Embassy Strategic Plan 2021-2022 Appendix J4 Occupational Health Strategy, and that Second Employee needed to move more, so he went into the kitchen and chased her round a bit, nipped her toes gently, and then stood right up on his back legs and hugged her knee. Esso said what should have happened then was, Second Employee should have recognised the unmistakeable (and indeed universal) Let's Play Chasey signal, chased him round the house, and, I quote, 'got her step count up and lost a few milimeters off that bum at the same time'.

What actually happened was, Second Employee shouted First Employee and utterly misrepresented Esso's helpful intervention by formally stating the following: 'Keith, help me, come and get this cat, he's biting my feet while I'm trying to drain the potatoes'. Then Esso was relocated by First Employee, who picked him up, kissed his head, and carried him upstairs with the words, Let's get you out of the way, Mr Naughty. Mr Naughty! I feel Esso has undermined our dignity as

Ambassadors, and, more worryingly, Second Employee got frustrated with him and said right that's it, if you nip my toes again I'm going to Withdraw Love from Both Of You. Ouch! Bloody Hell Esso! Well that's it, gone. No More Love. No More Love For Pussycats.

Well, it's not in Second Employee's job description to love anyone; and *actually* it's rather presumptuous of her and *I don't care anyway:* but on the other hand, if Second Employee doesn't love us any more, what will we do? I have been following her round, and she has stroked my whiskers back like normal and told me I am her tiny precious cat like she usually does: but what if she's just pretending, and is secretly intending to take us back to Cats' Protection tomorrow? Because we prefer it here, even though it does snow a lot. So, Esso and I have jointly decided to put Phase Two of the Occupational Health Strategy on hold, and we are going to look for a really nice present for Second Employee tonight. Hopefully that will smooth things over. When I was a very small kitten, I once brought a wood pigeon through the cat flap and First Employee especially has never stopped talking about it. So we're going to look for something even more impressive than that!

October 2021

Larry, and the Catinet. Esso here, Ambassador to the High Peak, updating on delivery of the High Peak Embassy Strategic

Plan 2021-2022. This week I've been working with Second Employee on a lace shawl we're both knitting for Second Employee's sister in law for Christmas. Second Employee does the twisty thing with the needles, and I provide the overall strategy. For example, earlier today I was saying, those S1K2togPSSOs look a bit sloppy, Second Employee, do you think you ought to tighten them up a bit. I take my role as co-creator very seriously. Sometimes at night, I take the shawl to the side of the sofa that Second Employee and I both share and sleep on it, carefully, and in the morning First Employee hinges me up and slides it out from underneath me while Second Employee wrings her hands and says, *eeuuurrgghh Keith be careful don't let him catch it with his Massive Claws!*

Ghost says she would never have employed Second Employee if she'd known she was a knitter, because 'you can't be trusted around wool, Esso'. Well, this is a terrible thing for Ghost to say, and completely untrue. She is thinking of the very minor incident a long time ago which everyone has forgotten because it was so incredibly minor. I mean I barely remember that it even happened. So obviously I don't have an *absolutely* clear recollection of events, but what I do remember is that, somehow, while I was bringing a ball of wool down three flights of stairs to look at it more closely, it fought back most unhelpfully: and it wasn't my fault at all, but *somehow* it ended up that there was an entire ball of wool unravelled all down the stairs, wrapped around every chair leg in the sitting room like an enormous spider web, and me tied up in the corner.

Luckily, Second Employee came in just before she had her morning shower, saw me, screamed, and rushed round, unravelling the entire ball of wool from the chair legs until she could free me. I was grateful, because it had been starting to feel quite tight around my Furry Middle. Unfortunately, Second Employee had no clothes on; because she had only been nipping out of the shower to get her towel, when she had seen the wool all the way down the stairs and followed it, intuiting, I really don't know how, that this was a situation which needed her input. There are two very large windows in our sitting room, one at each end. Second Employee said that nobody would have understood she was rescuing her cat who had tied himself up with Wool, and that, instead, the whole of the A6 between Buxton and Dove Holes must just have seen her running round the room naked, screeching like a banshee.

Ghost says that any combination of me and wool will eventually end badly and 'then it'll be who'd've thought it, Esso'. Well, I think Ghost slips too easily into the vernacular, and I also wonder what Ghost thinks she's going to be giving Second Employee's family for Christmas if not a nice shawl she's knitted, because we know from past experience that if you give them a proper present like a lovely big dead bird they scream!

October 2021

Larry, this is Ghost, Ambassador to the High Peak, reporting on diplomatic progress. Well, things have gone very, very wrong this weekend. Firstly, Second Employee has put her terrible painting in a frame, and is going to hang the bloody thing in the hall. I tried my best to discourage her: I investigated the Frame Packaging and I decided to ATTACK. I did a proper bottom-wiggle pounce at it and everything, but she was UNMOVED. She said, look Ghost, remember I had to move that other one so it's just going in its place. Well, Second Employee, we don't *actually* have a quota for pictures in the hall, and I don't think the world will end if we have seven rather than eight in your gallery wall. Larry, could you please pass a law which will make Second Employee take that terrible picture down and paint the hall a neutral colour. Esso says I am Politically Naive and you can't just pass laws like that, 'it will have to be a white paper first Ghost or a green paper or something similar'. Well, whatever, Larry, let's get it done together, it will benefit all of us if Employees are given proper boundaries.

Secondly, First Employee has taken to singing 'The Esso sign means happy motoring' to Esso, which is nonsense, because 'Esso', *as we all know*, means The Noble One, or Scourge of Voles, although it is a good job it means that already because if it was based on Esso himself it would have to mean 'Sleeps A Lot and Purrs'.

Thirdly, and most seriously, Second Employee escaped this morning and ran a thing called a '10K' in Sheffield with a lot of other silly people. I'm not entirely sure what this involves, but Esso, who was in charge at the time and should have intervened, said it mostly involved a lot of lycra, and it is his informed belief that she went to Sheffield and ran round and round and round a park until she fell over. Why anyone would do this, we do not know. In any case, things are serious. The best thing about Second Employee - indeed, one might say, the only good thing, but that would be perhaps a little unfair - is her doughy middle which both Esso and I enjoy kneading. We do not want her to do anything which might tone it up. I was very annoyed with Esso, because he should have stopped them going out: he said, and I quote, he just 'thought they were making an early start on going to Aldi'. Well, Esso and I both know that the trip to Aldi involves 3 coffees at least and a 20 minute argument about whether they should start having a veg box, so why he thought they would bypass that on this Sunday of all Sundays *I do not know*. But Esso says we should not worry too much, because we know that Second Employee can barely take the bins out without eating a big slice of cake afterwards, and she would have finished that 10k and been 'straight down the nearest cafe, mainlining a cappuccino and a scone'. Well, I have made sure to do some extensive exploratory kneading this afternoon, and I think Esso was quite correct. But I do not quite consider us entirely out of danger yet, and I will be monitoring the situation extremely carefully over the coming days!

October 2021

Dear Larry and the Catinet. This is Esso here, a very worried Ambassador to the High Peak, having a bad day. I'm currently Pretending to Relax on the sofa with all my Leggies in the air, in an admirable display of Sangfroid: but actually things are rather challenging. I've upset Ghost unintentionally; and now she's FUROUS with me.

I had a quiet word with her about the amount of time she spends following Second Employee about and kneading on her; because Second Employee is unproductive at the best of times, and to be fair to her, it must make it more difficult to get on with things if she's got Ghost continually following her around and weaving under her feet. For example; Second Employee has been trying to tidy the coat rack for three days, and she still hasn't managed it. I mean, it's hardly much of an ambition to start with, is it? What if Second Employee gets run over by a bus tomorrow? What will her eulogy say? She tried to tidy up the coat rack but her cat kept squeaking at her and she gave up? I really don't think we can have that. Anyway, I said to Ghost, look Ghost, I know we can get attached to the Employees, it's quite understandable. We had to leave Mother when we were still very young, didn't we, and so the lure of something warm and furry is difficult to give up, and Second Employee does have all those dodgy cashmere jumpers in the wrong size she gets cheap from Label Traders. So I'm not judging you, Ghost, but for God's sake leave her alone for a bit and we might finally get the pan drawer sorted out, and if you can hold off for a day or two she might even get round to moving the shoe cupboard.

Anyway, Ghost took it badly. I mean really, really badly. She said if I thought she was the type to become emotionally reliant on an Ape then I had another think coming. She said *she* didn't care anyway if Second Employee *did* get run over by a bus, and she, Ghost, would do her eulogy, and it would say, Second Employee was incapable of planning a gallery wall or painting anything a sensible colour 'and that would blow that whole situation wide open'. Well! I honestly don't know where we go from here. Ghost says she's requesting a transfer to Derbyshire Dales and she's sacking Second Employee anyway and I've got to tell her tonight. It really is difficult. I'm just going to let things settle down for a little bit and hope Ghost gets over it. I'm not going to rock the boat. I might just see if Ghost is a bit more amenable later, and remind her we're coming up to the Happy Cold Times, when First Employee makes the fire in the sitting room work especially for us, and they put on the Festival Of Cat Toys Tied To A Tree. Ghost loves the Festival Of Cat Toys Tied To A Tree! Yes, I'll go and remind her about that. I'm sure that'll make her reconsider!

October 2021

Larry and the Catinet. This is Ghost, Ambassador to the High Peak, updating you on developments.

Esso hurt my feelings very badly the other day. He implied - in fact, Larry, he more than implied, he actually came straight out and said it - that I have become emotionally dependent on Second Employee. Me! A noble, independent Feline, attached to the - the *staff*! I think not! Well, I was so cross I ignored Esso, First and Second Employee, Grey Next Door Cat and the entirety of the North Buxton Monochrome Cat Alliance (even though they were trying to get me to confirm the minutes of last week's meeting) for at least six hours. At least! I sat upstairs writing my Transfer Request letter, and also my exposé to send to the Daily Bone (don't push me, Esso, I know what happened to that elephant ornament that 'got lost' 2 years ago), when Esso came to fetch me in a panic.

While I'd been MANIPULATED and GUILTED into taking my constant eye off Second Employee she'd bought a new sideboard and *moved our scratchy boxes* to get it in. Moved our scratchy boxes! To *another part of the room*! Well. All I can say is, disasters happen when my very pure and noble motives are misconstrued, and I've been persuaded to resume my close and absolutely constant supervision. And it was lucky that I did, because I was able to fix Second Employee with my Very Firm

Judgy Expression when I saw her going on eBay. No more Denby bloody Arabesque, Second Employee, if you hadn't 'started a little ceramics collection' we wouldn't have needed that sideboard to start with and I'd have my transfer to Derbyshire Dales by now!

October 2021

Larry and the Catinet: Esso here, Ambassador to the High Peak, checking in. This is an Action Briefing, right from the middle of a Diplomatic Mission: imagine me running into the Sitting Room and my co-Ambassador Ghost rushing up to Sniff Noses and Debrief. Unfortunately if you were to imagine the scene accurately you would notice that Second Employee's Large Hairy Cardigan is in the way: but there we are, that's Second Employee all over, making everything less glamorous than it needs to be. Anyway, I can't say much about my mission at the moment, but I will tell you that it involves some very complex negotiations with Chunky Black Cat down the road who's been trying to move in to this house, and I'm expecting a breakthrough shortly. He said to me, look, Esso, you've got four floors in that house, I shall have at least one of them. Can you imagine the cheek of him?! Quite unbelievable. Well, I'd like to see him look Ghost in the eye and tell her that, because she took over the top floor for her sole use the day she moved in, and she brooks no opposition. I shall report back on developments.

I'd also like to report that it was Second Employee's birthday yesterday. In the interest of keeping good relations with the staff, we very carefully considered the things we most appreciated about her - biscuit provision and stroking - , and we wrote them on a card. We had to do it via First Employee, because of the UTTER RIDICULOUSNESS of us not having opposable thumbs. And let me tell you, opposable thumbs have been wasted on First Employee. His handwriting is terrible. It is execrable. It is incomprehensible. Ghost and I have discussed the matter, and we would like to swap First Employee for one who can write properly, please. What if he were ever needed to write an Emergency Catnip Requisition Memo?! I mean, we haven't ever revisited the recruitment criteria for either of the Employees because, Larry, we don't like to cast aspersions on Diplomatic Recruitment Procedures, but, frankly, we think the whole thing needs revisiting. We need new procedures and a wider pool of applicants. This writing thing is pushing us too far. He is mocking us with his inadequate opposable thumb usage! We await his replacement eagerly!

October 2021

Hello Larry. Ghost here, Ambassador for the High Peak updating you on progress. I am writing this from under my special radiator on the top floor of the Embassy, which is my personal floor belonging solely to me and Esso agrees entirely that it is completely mine. I certainly wouldn't have painted the landing wall yellow, especially with that carpet, but I'm afraid Second Employee has always been unusually stubborn in that regard. I honestly think her Farrow And Ball Paint Chart is missing some of its sections; because I've never known her go anywhere near a Sophisticated Cool Neutral in the entire time she's been working for me. Perhaps she thinks she's allergic. Esso doesn't come up here because he's too lazy to climb up all the stairs, but he chirrups at me from the floor below if there are important diplomatic developments he needs to update me on: like Grey Next Door Cat going back on the Great Territory Negotiations of 2019, which I'm very, very sad to say has happened this week.

I do allow the Employees to share this floor a little bit. They have a room they sleep in which I have NO interest in going into at night, thank you, so First Employee can shut the door all he wants and I don't care, as if he isn't going to walk past me ninety three times between 1am and 7am anyway because of his dodgy prostate! Sometimes Second Employee hides in there in the daytime as well, especially if we have people staying. She hasn't had my diplomatic training, and can't sustain a conversation about how awful the weather is in Buxton and can it really be as bad as it seems for more than three hours at a stretch. When she does, I wait for her to lie down on the bed, so I can sit on her chest and stare into her eyes. She says it's a good job she hasn't got a guilty conscience, because if she had, she would find that level of scrutiny very disturbing. Good. Think about that, Second Employee, next time you think about buying sideboards and moving my scratchy box. Think about that.

October 2021

Larry and the Catinet. Esso here, Ambassador to the High Peak. I and Ghost (mainly me. It was my idea) have a diplomatic success to report. I had a Brilliant Thought the other week. I was taking part in Second Employee's Zoom French Conversation class, and it was exactly like all the other things Second Employee does on Zoom, a lot of people on a screen moaning about how tired they are, only this time in French. However! It did make me think. I thought, here is Second Employee, trying her best to talk to people in a different language (although as I said to Ghost, I think the only verb she can actually conjugate in the subjunctive is pouvoir, and where's that going to get her?) and yet we've never tried to teach her Cat! I know you'll all agree: we cats always think the Apes are too stupid for The True Language. I used to find it slightly poignant watching Second Employee continually google, why do my cats never miaow? (Although actually that wasn't entirely true, Ghost did miaow once, in 2019, to stop Second Employee trapping her head in a drawer, due to her having put her head in the drawer just as it was being closed.) Anyway, Ghost said she is the linguist in this family and she would really put her mind to it and see where she can get with things: and she's managed to teach Second Employee the following three phrases:

Brrrrrrp (rising intonation): I note that something is occurring over here, and I feel I should be involved.
Brrrrrrp (falling intonation): I'm not interested. I'm asleep. Tell me later.
Brrrrrrp! (staccato): Stop pulling burrs out of my tail! Go and do it to Esso instead!

(Although I do slightly query Ghost's translation of the second half of that last one).

Well, Larry, it's been a blinding success. Second Employee can understand all of those phrases consistently now, although admittedly when she tries to say them back to us her pronunciation is terrible. I'm now working with her on the sound sequence for 'I, a CAT, have entered the room!' and we've probably got about 70% recognition. We're rather proud of her.

Now, we have considered the downside, which is that, theoretically, Second Employee may at some point in the future be able to walk along the street and understand what cats say privately to each other. But, she really does have a very, very small brain, and we think there's very little chance of her getting much further. So Ghost says, she's going to persevere, because she thinks clear communication is very important, and there are a number of things she'd like to say to Second Employee without any room for misinterpretation: like, could you go to Morrisons and buy us a Dressed Crab immediately; is the Festival of Cat Toys Tied To A Tree going to be soon; please tell First Employee to stop playing that awful miserable thing on the piano; and we really don't think those dungarees do you any favours. The one about the dungarees I actually think we need to say sooner rather than later, so we're concentrating on teaching her that. Honestly, this could be a real breakthrough in feline-ape relations. We'll keep you all posted!

[Note from Esso: it is one of the few regrets of my time in office that we have so far failed to convey adequately to Second Employee quite how much those dungarees do not do her any favours. Indeed, we rather hit a low last year when she bought some new bottle-green corduroy ones. I think we will resume our efforts.]

November 2021

Larry and the Catinet: Esso here, Ambassador to the High Peak. I'm truly sorry to report that Second Employee is causing us Issues again, although it's possible I started her off on her current unfortunate path. It's cold here at the moment, so when I come in of an evening I like to sit and knead on her doughy middle. It warms my feet up, conditions my muscles, and lets me get some purring done, so it's useful, but Second Employee says she never realised quite how doughy her middle was until I started doing it. Then the final straw came one day when she was napping on the Top Floor Bed with Ghost, and Ghost was under her arm purring. Suddenly, and very creditably, Ghost remembered she'd scheduled some talks with Black and White Cat From The Back Lane which she was almost late for; and, unusually for Ghost I might add, felt a sense of responsibility; so she leapt vertically up in the air, and used Second Employee's stomach as a trampoline to get her off the bed quicker.

Well, Second Employee said it ends here and enough is enough and lots of other unhelpful things, and the upshot of it is, now she's doing yoga over Zoom every day. Obviously, Ghost is having to supervise and help her with her alignment, and she's exhausted. Ghost says Second Employee stepped back from Bird of Paradise into Warrior 2 one day and her back foot was so far off that who knows what would have happened if Ghost hadn't been waiting, ready to reposition her with her claws; and, unbelievably, she wasn't grateful at all. In fact, she screamed and fell over!

Second Employee sometimes tells us about the Before Times when she lived in Difficult Circumstances, and used to go running round and round and round in the dark to delay having to go back to her house. She says, she might have been miserable, but she looked amazing and had lots of energy, so

Ghost and I have got to be supportive with the yoga. But Larry, we don't want to be supportive! What would be the point of Second Employee looking AMAZING in a small town in the middle of miles of trees and mountains? Who is she going to AMAZE? She's not going to amaze us! We're very worldly wise. Personally, I wasn't even amazed when First 'I only watch edgy drama with subtitles' Employee became addicted to Bake Off, because I think we'd all seen that one coming for a long time. Likewise, what is the point of her having lots of energy, when all she does when she has a burst of energy is paint another room purple, and besides, we like her lying down a lot so we can nap on her?

So, Larry, with your agreement we would like to add a few more points to Second Employee's Job Description: 1/ To maintain doughy middle in at least current state in order to facilitate feline kneading and warming of feet and 2/ To restrict Zoom Yoga to one hour per week as it causes Ghost a lot of work, and also she needs to do some fairly rigorous CPD on fascias and Yoga Nidra before she really feels confident.

Thank you Larry, I really think this will help enormously in keeping the Ambassadorial Residence a relaxed and happy place!

November 2021

Larry and the Catinet: this is Ghost here, Ambassador to the High Peak, updating you on my TRIUMPH. Well, Esso said it couldn't be done and I was wasting my time, but I did it and I think you'll agree that I should get my transfer to a nice cottage in the Derbyshire Dales (painted neutrally throughout) immediately. Yes… I've been teaching First Employee to speak Cat! If you remember, I'd had some success teaching Second Employee a few phrases. I'm extremely pleased with her progress: but Esso says that, thinking about it, *actually* Second Employee is the kind of person who teaches herself Sanskrit for fun rather than doing anything constructive, like, for example, painting the outside furniture with wood preserver, or making money: so it was not that much of a achievement. Well more fool you then Esso, because I've taught both of them!

This is how it happened. I'd been getting increasingly frustrated with First Employee. He's recently become addicted to Bake Off, and when he watched the one last week he got quite upset and said 'why do they have to keep going and have a winner? Why can't they just stop now. They're all lovely.' Well, I really felt at that point that he needed input from someone experienced and realistic, perhaps a bit cynical: like me, for example, because obviously Second Employee is useless in that regard. So, I've been patiently talking to him, (and he's been 'so surprised at how chatty little Ghostycat is suddenly!')

and I won't quite say he's got a full grasp of conjugations, but he's starting to be able to pick out phrases.

Esso and I have discussed the issue, and we have a number of things we would like to say to First Employee now he can almost understand the One True Language. The first one is, could you keep your voice down, please. This is our major gripe with First Employee: indeed, Second Employee once got frustrated with him and said 'Love, you're asking me if I want a cup of tea, not giving your final Lear from the stage of the Old Vic'. Second Employee is not often right, but on this occasion she was, so at least the neighbours didn't all hear his opinions on every single article in the Guardian that morning. Also, Esso says he is convinced First Employee is actually a Secret Criminal, and that is why he's been exiled to the High Peak, because he's always moaning about the cold so we're sure he can't have come here willingly. So we would like to ask him, what is the nature of your crime, because having seen you FAFFING trying to rescue all those mice we bring in and keep them alive we think you would have been a rubbish murderer. So what is it. Esso says, next time we will not have Rescue Employees with dubious pasts, we will have expensive pedigree ones; but for the moment we have got to make do.

Also, on an exciting note - Esso says Second Employee was showing him a new cat toy earlier that she's bought for the Festival Of Cat Toys Tied To A Tree. It must be soon! I'm so excited. Last year I really worked on my moves, and I swiped so many cat toys off the tree for Esso and me to play with that Second Employee was still finding them all summer. This year I'm going for gold - those special vintage 50s glass cat toys Second Employee puts right at the top of the Big Tree in the sitting room. I'm in training already. Watch this space!

November 2021

Larry and the Catinet; it's a very sad and disappointed Esso here, Ambassador to the High Peak. Well, I imagine you've heard all the rumours by now about Ghost's terrible behaviour yesterday; I know the WhatsApp groups have been Quite Agog. I imagine it's been all over Twitter. So I thought I should get in touch to give you the full, unadulterated story.

It wasn't as if Second Employee hadn't warned us, more than once, that we had to go to the vet to have our weight checked so they could make sure we were on the right flea medication; but I *personally* don't think Ghost thought the Employees would actually go ahead with it. Well: the Cat Carriers of Doom came out of the shed, and First Employee scooped us up and put us in: as you know, I'm a very stoical cat, and I dealt with it admirably. But Ghost! Oh my *Lord*. The minute the door closed, Ghost began with a full-throated rendition of the Ballad Of The Disgruntled Kitten. I mean, I tried to shout across to her to tell her it was deeply inappropriate, but she carried on. First and

Second Employee stuffed us in the Small Grey Peugeot, and Second Employee sat in the back to talk to us: and, Larry, this is what surprised me. When Ghost and I had our diplomatic training, they said to us, if, during your diplomatic efforts, the High Peak residents do something embarrassing and gauche, you must do it too, to make them feel comfortable. If they drink the finger bowl, you drink it too. If they carry on going outside and pretending the High Peak is habitable, despite it having rained for sixty days solid, you do it too. Well, who knew Second Employee had had the same training? So when Ghost began the Ballad, which as you know, Larry, is a shameful thing to do now we are no longer kittens, Second Employee joined in. So we had Ghost with her rather fine mezzo-soprano, and Second Employee having a relatively creditable go at the alto part. I thought I might as well join in with my tenor. Larry, it was actually rather moving, especially the rousing chorus, which we all sang together in harmony as we went round the roundabout near Morrisons: Mi-aaaaooow! Mi-aaaaaoooow! Oh! Mi-OOOOOOO! Mi-OOOOOO!

But I'm afraid, Larry, it got worse. At the vet, the nice nurse went to give us our flea treatment, and Ghost said very clearly, and I quote: 'Well, you can stick that awful stuff right up your bum Lady, because I'm not having it'. Larry, I was horrified, and I am just so glad that we haven't yet taught Second Employee Advanced Colloquial Cat, because I don't think she entirely understood, and I think I was able to distract everyone sufficiently. Imagine, though! Ghost could have undone all my good work of the last two years! I've spoken to her, and she's pretending to be unrepentant! She says she wasn't frightened at all, she just suddenly felt we all needed more music in our lives and that the Ballad Of The Disgruntled Kitten was due for a revival: and also, since the only person in this house who's ever actually been bitten by a flea is Second Employee, why isn't she the one getting the horrible flea treatment and not us. Well, I think Ghost just needs to settle a bit and she'll see the error of her ways, but I would request, Larry, that she doesn't get her transfer to Derbyshire Dales quite yet. I think she needs to be where I can keep an eye on her. Especially given that Second Employee managed to get the Vet appointment a bit confused and we've got to go back again next week for a 'full check up and a booster'. I honestly quail at the thought of telling Ghost. But then I think of my diplomatic training and I think, come on Esso, stiff upper lip, think of England. We're doing it for the greater good!

November 2021

Larry and the Catinet, Ghost and Esso here, Ambassadors to the High Peak. We need to discuss something with you as a matter of the utmost urgency: Second Employee is decorating again! Larry, we need emergency legislation to stop her. At least she's used a slightly more subtle colour this time after her Uncontested Aesthetic Nadir which was the orange dining room, but she was telling First Employee about trying to buy the paint, and it didn't sound to us like she's built any bridges at all with the High Peak inhabitants. It was a terrible thing when Second Employee discovered she could get any Farrow and Ball paint shade copied at the shop down the road: because it she'd had to pay the money to buy the real thing it would have stopped her. Anyway apparently she was trying to buy a copy of something called 'Sulking Room Pink' and she couldn't make the man who does the mixing understand, so she stood there bellowing, No! Sulking Room! *Sulking* Room! until finally the man looked it up on his phone and said accusingly, Ah, SULKing room, and now Second Employee feels her accent has been Disrespected, 'although my family are documented as having been *in this literal area* since the Bubonic Plague, and I personally am Derbyshire born and bred apart from those 20 years in the Fens which clearly *ruined my vowels*'. Second Employee says she is going to go and try to buy Four Candles next, which is ridiculous, because we have got a lot of candles already, and in fact last time we had visitors for dinner she said to First Employee, Darling, can you go and light the candelabra, and everyone laughed at her: even though we actually have got a candelabra, which Second Employee got cheap on eBay, and which is enormous, because she read the measurements wrong. So Larry, could you pass some Bills or Laws or Green Papers or whatever they are please. First, to stop Second Employee going out to shops and asking for ridiculous things and upsetting the locals. And Second, to make Second Employee recognise that she is terrible at choosing colours and cutting in, and we would like a proper qualified person to come and paint the house a very pale greige throughout. Thank you Larry. We also think it would also be helpful if both our employees received some additional training in diplomacy, as we honestly cannot be with them all the time, although Ghost tries, and the potential for them causing trouble is huge!

November 2021

Larry, Ghost here, Ambassador to the High Peak, notifying you that Second Employee has worn me out - worn me out! with her ridiculous decorating of rooms in Sulking Room Pink when we were all busy enough already, and her making of Things Involving Sultanas and Brandy which *apparently* 'don't need your nose in them, Mrs Nosy Pussy Cat'. So I am leaving Second Employee to her grating of nutmegs and boiling things for hours and swearing, and I am conserving my energy under my radiator. Perhaps in my absence, instead of cornering the market in producing lace doilies and things in jars, Second Employee might develop a skill which actually contributes to the sum of human knowledge or makes some money: but I'm not hopeful. Esso and I have decided we're really going to double down with her Workplan in the New Year. Yes - we think it might be time for Second Employee to be given some proper Strategic Aims and be monitored against KPIs!

November 2021

Larry and the Catinet, Ghost here, Ambassador to the High Peak, updating you on what a very, very brave and dignified cat I am. Esso may have mentioned a while ago about when our employees took us to the Vet, and at the same time, coincidentally and quite unaccountably, my mouth began to sing the Ballad Of The Disgruntled Kitten. No-one knows why this happened: Esso and I both agree it is a mystery. I had been lost in musings when it began, about how we were perhaps not really going to the Vet, but being transferred FINALLY to Derbyshire Dales: and how, if that was the case, would there be an empty space forever under my radiator, or would a new Ambassador be brought in: and would Second Employee stroke the new Ambassador and tell her she was the softest and most precious cat in the whole of Buxton while I was sitting all on my own in Bakewell, un-stroked and unloved. And that was when it started. So I don't know why it happened, but I think actually it was my subconscious wanting to show First Employee what proper music is, especially since Esso heard him telling someone recently that he thought Prog Rock was underrated. Anyway, due to Second Employee having messed up the appointment situation we have been to the Vet AGAIN, but this time my mouth did not sing the Ballad Of The Disgruntled Kitten, and Esso said, what is going on with you over there, Ghost, have you fainted in shock. But I had not. The shock was to come later, and Larry, I would like you to treat this letter as a formal complaint. When we got to the Vet, we both had to come out of our boxes one after another so we could be admired, and I came out first, and the Vet said, hasn't she got the most beautiful markings on her fur, which I have; so that was correct, and well observed. But when Esso came out he said, 'My Goodness! Haven't you got A PRESENCE!' and Larry, I really think it is more appropriate for an Ambassador to have a PRESENCE than even very very beautiful markings, and he should have said that about me, too. So could you ask Second Employee to challenge comments like this if I ever have to go the Vet again. Thank you.

And could you also say to Second Employee, next time she is telling cats they have to go to the Vet, she might want to remember to tell them they will also be coming back: and that way, things will go more smoothly, and with fewer ballads. We met a Mrs Whiskers as we came out, who was a good 3/4 of the way through a very spirited rendition of the Aria des Félins Furieux from the Opéra des Chats: we were able to explain the situation to her, and she decided to finish her Aria another time. What good luck Esso and I are always there to compensate for the inadequacies of Employees, and to bring diplomacy and proper organisation to the High Peak!

November 2021

Larry and the Catinet, Esso here, Ambassador to the High Peak. I just wondered if I could talk to you a little bit about Second Employee. Because actually I wondered if you could put her in a Catalogue Of Embassy Staff or similar so we could swap her for a better one. We've been snowed in all weekend, and instead of doing anything at all sensible like, for example, a proper stock take of the Royal Canin Biscuits, she's painted the dining room fuchsia. Larry, we can't live like this. Ghost heard her once telling First Employee she 'makes sure she goes to different paint shops so they don't realise how many colours she's using', and even First Employee, who hasn't got the sense he was born with, told her that was a questionable road to go down since it's exactly what he used to do with Gin before he gave up Wild Living and Hedonism and Being Difficult. Ghost and I have discussed the issue and we really feel it's Too Much: we know you wanted us to rehabilitate Rescue Employees, but we could get so much more done if we had nice pedigree ones! Could you get us some proper ones sent, please? We are very close to the station: Ghost thinks there is a fast train from London to Chesterfield, although after that we are a little bit hazy. They will need to supply their own big coats, and enjoy being kneaded with claws. Many thanks. Ghost and I await your convenience!

Chapter 4

Winter 21/22: The Polar Night Approaches

December 2021

Larry and the Catinet. It's Esso here, Ambassador to the High Peak, with my update.

Well, Larry, it's been a difficult week here, and everyone's feelings are hurt. My feelings are hurt because I have *twice* tried to do a good deed for Second Employee and my efforts have been unappreciated. For example: I was helping her the other night to see what the fibre content might be of a particular and rather interesting ball of wool. Just at the point when I was concluding that it had no nylon and so wouldn't be ideal for socks - would you believe, at such a moment of insight - First Employee distracted me by tickling my tummy, and *took my wool away*? Disgraceful. And, in addition, I attended Second Employee's last Zoom Yoga session with her to help her refine her practice: I stretched myself all down the length of her yoga mat, to encourage her, and when she did her 'downward dog' (ridiculous name) on top of me I could see quite clearly that her nose was in the wrong position: so I bit it. Larry, she relocated me into the hallway! And she let Ghost stay in the room! And Ghost was asleep, so she was being no help at all with Alignment, like I was! I don't like to accuse Second Employee of blatant favouritism since we are really very good friends and possibly Best Friends, but I just set those neutral facts before you and let you judge for yourselves.

[Note from Esso: I would like to reiterate that Second Employee and I really are Very Best Friends, and I continue to forgive her any minor infractions such as this.]

Ghost's feelings are hurt too, because Ghost's feelings are always hurt about something or other, because, frankly, she wanders about looking for something to take offence at, and, when one does that, one usually finds it. But, First Employee's feelings are hurt too, which has surprised Ghost and I; because we had no idea he had any feelings. He certainly doesn't look as if he does! But Ghost heard him saying to Second Employee 'and when they (we presume that is us) come into a room and I'm in it on my own, they look disappointed and walk out again. Why do they prefer you? What's wrong with me?' Well, of course, we are strictly professional Ambassadors who have no attachment to anyone, but I will just say that First Employee really does have a very, very loud voice, and wherever we are we can hear him bellowing something: normally, 'Susie, what floor are you on? Do you want a coffee?' or, 'My God, Susie, can you believe it's snowing again?'; whereas Second Employee has a very soft voice, and is always sitting about on chairs for long enough for us to find her and get some really productive kneading in.

So the only one of us who has not got hurt feelings at the moment is Second Employee, because her brain really is very, very tiny, and she does not know we asked you to put her in the Catalogue Of Failed Employees so we could get someone better. She must never find out. Larry, I am sorry: I spoke in anger and exasperation. We must keep the Employees, despite their faults. They are our moral responsibility, and we haven't yet given up on the possibility of training them up to be Better People: and also, Ghost says, it is just too poignant to think of asking Second Employee to leave in this cold weather. Where would she go? Would she have to wander about on the moors, like a wraith, so far from her natural habitat which we understand to be the Cambridge John Lewis? As far as we have ever been able to tell, Second Employee's only survival skill is the ability to find somewhere that sells a cappuccino and a pastry in almost any situation: we think in this weather, and this landscape, even that poor skill might fail her. No, Larry, we will all go on together: and whatever the personal cost to Ghost and I, we will bear it!

December 2021

Hello Larry and the Catinet. This is Ghost here, Ambassador to the High Peak, with my update. Esso says I have to do this update 'because I've done the last few and they'll think you do nothing but lounge about under your radiator, Ghost', but I'm a very, very busy cat at the moment, and honestly, I've barely got the time. I really can barely even convey in words how busy I've been. Second Employee and I have been preparing for the Festival Of Cat Toys Tied To A Tree - so much fun! It's been quite emotional, getting out all the familiar toys, many still with our teeth marks on. How happy we've been, smacking them off the tree and chasing them triumphantly under the sofa!

Now, Larry, you may want to sit down for this, because I've got something very, very interesting to tell you. I've been doing some research, and I've discovered that the Employees don't only celebrate the Festival. No! Imagine! They have other funny little things they celebrate at the same time! So far, this is what I've gleaned. Towards the end of the Festival, lots of the Employees here in the High Peak have their own special day, called Christy-Maus, or Christmas. I'm not entirely sure what this involves, but through careful observation of where Second Employee has been expending her energies recently I think it must be about everyone properly appreciating her Pudding, because it took her eight hours to steam it and we've not heard the end of it yet.

Esso says this is actually not true, the Pudding is incidental: he has been talking to Grey Cat Next Door, who has told him it is *actually* a ritual where families come together, eat a lot of cheese, and tell each other what they really think of each other. I don't know why we need a special day for this, because we all know what Second Employee's Mother thinks of everyone anyway, especially Esso. Second Employee has purchased a Knitted Replica of a family on eBay, who are all standing round looking at the one who is too young to criticise anyone yet. She has placed it very carefully underneath a painting of her and First Employee's God, which is a Large White Cat which she apparently 'bought while we were living in the Fens'. Esso says he is not sure the white cat is actually their God, as Second Employee has form for buying quite random paintings, and we have 'not yet got enough data to form a proper conclusion, Ghost' but Larry, she has arranged her Replica Family right underneath the painting, next to the Lava Lamp, so you can appreciate how clear it is what Second Employee has done, and how silly Esso is being.

And that is not all. Other people celebrate things other than Christy-Maus or Christmas! We actually think there might be many things! We know Second Employee celebrates something called The Solstice. This is mainly about eating cake. We do not know what Interim Summer Employee celebrates: we know he is something called A Satanist, but First Employee says this is *actually* something called An Affectation, and he will grow out of it just like he grew out of Ayn Rand.

I'm sure you'll agree, Larry, that my update has been much more useful than Esso's are, because it has actual facts backed up by objective, scientific research. Esso says I have not got to ask for my transfer to Derbyshire Dales today and I have got to 'give it a bit of a rest, Ghost, for God's sake', but I have decided to leave it until after the Festival anyway, as everything is very interesting at the moment. But don't forget how clever I am, Larry, when the time comes. I hope you're having a lovely Festival too!

December 2021

Larry and the Catinet, Esso here, Ambassador to the High Peak, with my Festival Of Cat Toys Tied To A Tree Update. Larry: I'm afraid things are going rather badly, and we may have to ask for your assistance. It appears that the Employees cannot be trusted to celebrate Christy-Maus Christmas Yule in an appropriate fashion. First Employee has brought a thing of terror into this house. I wish I could attach a video; but if I were able, I would be forced to advise you only to watch it in bright daylight and in sensible company. It is very hard to describe. Ghost says she has heard it called a 'snow globe'; it is large and lights up and rotates while playing Christmas Songs, although it does not, mercifully, do any of these things for long, because Second Employee has stated for the record that it 'gets through batteries at a rate of knots, especially the dodgy cheap ones First Employee bought from Lomas Stores instead of Waitrose'. Ghost heard First Employee saying to Second Employee that it was 'probably the best Fifteen Pounds that anyone has spent on anything, ever': well, Larry, we beg to differ. We are not entirely sure how much Fifteen Pounds is in real money: Ghost thinks it is the amount Second Employee spends on Cake in a day, whereas I am fairly sure it is a tiny bit more than the Employees spent on the Ambassadorial Residence in total: but however much it is, it is too much to spend on that horror. We are not quite sure how to deal with this, Larry, but I am going to try to kill it before my next report, in case it snatches away our souls. I will keep you updated.

Furthermore, and I report this more in sorrow than in anger: Second Employee's mother appears to have become confused about the actual date of Christy-Maus Christmas, which we understand is in a few weeks, and has already performed the ritual of Families Telling Each Other What They Think Of Them. This is very difficult for everyone, Larry, especially Second Employee's Mother, because now she will have to think up a lot more things to say for Christmas proper. This is why it is not good to do things on the wrong day, but to have self-control and wait until the appointed time. Moreover, Second Employee has become Maudlin, and says that when she lived in the miserable place, before she was lucky enough to be employed by us alongside First Employee, she used to get through Christmas by going running at night and looking through people's windows at their beautiful trees and their cats: and she thought that, one day, she would have a beautiful tree in a window and beautiful cats too. So she has put ours there to encourage anyone else who is running round, being miserable on purpose through a lack of emotional rectitude. Well, Larry, we think Second Employee has completely misjudged this whole affair, because if anyone is robust enough to be running about in Buxton at this time of year for whatever reason they will be far too hardened to care about aesthetics, and in the meantime we can't close the curtains properly; although Ghost is enjoying sitting on the windowsill and launching herself at the Cat Toys.

[Note from Esso: Second Employee, it turned out, could not cope with the aesthetics of the Tree in the Window and was forced to make First Employee move it all to its normal place behind the television. Ghost adapted admirably. She simply started from a position directly underneath it and POUNCED.]

We think, Larry, that the Employees need the rules for Christmas to be formally reiterated. We wondered if your employee - the one who does the updates on TV occasionally about Bad Corvids (a very real problem here in the High Peak: we are overwhelmed with very awkward Jackdaws, particularly) could do a brief explanation so they all understand what is required of them. Namely, unfettered access to the Trees for the Festival of Cat Toys Tied To A Tree, and Christmas celebrations to be kept restrained and only on the one day. In particular, all revolving snow globe HORRORS to be placed in a large hole and left. We believe there are a number of large holes and caves down the road in Castleton, presumably for this purpose.

Thank you Larry, and we will try our best at this end to model decent standards of behaviour for the Employees too!

December 2021

Larry and the Catinet. Ghost here, Joint Ambassador to the High Peak, updating you on what an excellent Employer I am. I was explaining to Second Employee earlier that when she is very, very tired because of Boosters and Depressing Corvids and there being no daylight now in the High Peak until next April, she is right to hide away in the bedroom from Esso: because if she lies on the sofa downstairs he will not leave her alone, and jumps on her and wakes her up and kneads her middle very, very firmly. She is much better off lying down in the bedroom, with me, so I can get some good firm kneading done on her arm. It is actually Second Employee's duty to keep herself in reasonable energy and health, because she's not very dynamic at the best of times, and ideally we'd like her to be a bit more productive. I explained this to her while I was kneading, then I went off to check on my radiator and came back and jumped on her and kneaded again a couple more times. I think it helped her feel more optimistic and focused. Although when she went downstairs afterwards I did hear her saying 'Goodness me, you again, Esso, haven't you got big claws', rather faintly, so I think there is still work for Second Employee to do on Assertiveness. I will suggest to Esso that we add it to her workplan for next year - although her workplan is getting rather long!

December 2021

Larry and the Catinet. Ghost here, Ambassador to the High Peak, with an *extremely* worrying update. Larry, I will come straight out and say it: Second Employee has gone mad. We think we are keeping the situation under control: Esso follows her if she is in the kitchen or the sitting room, and sits behind her with his cheek against hers, purring and monitoring everything she is doing. If she ventures into the upper floors I'm there, kneading away and keeping her sitting still and calm for as long as possible. Between us, we make sure she's *never alone*, despite her mutterings that she is 'an introvert' and 'no-one understands how difficult it is'.

Introvert! What nonsense! Esso and I don't believe in Silly Introverts any more than First Employee does! Luckily my radiator is right outside her and First Employee's bedroom, so I can monitor the situation throughout the night, although last night I suffered terribly - terribly! Because my radiator went off, and I had to wait for First Employee to get up and re-pressure the boiler. Luckily he is always lurking about at night, monitoring things and looking for something to organise, so I didn't wait for long; but it was a difficult thirty minutes, I can tell you, especially in Buxton where the temperature can drop to a level that endangers life in the time it takes to make a cup of coffee or, more relevantly, fill up a bowl with biscuits!

Anyway. Second Employee has announced that actually she 'can't deal' with Christmas because 'it has got too many difficult memories', and she has not iced the cake yet. It is our understanding, Larry, and of course do correct me if I'm mistaken, that the employees aren't allowed to be going about 'not dealing' with Christmas: they have to get their tinsel and their marzipan out and crack on with it. Then she said she might as well live in Finland where 'at least they are geared up to the Polar Night', and told Esso she was going to learn Finnish and that would show everyone. Well, it would certainly show Esso, because he has trouble even with understanding Grey Next Door Cat's accent, because he says Grey Cat has never pronounced an H since we met him. Larry, then it got worse. Esso says she has been on her laptop while he has been laying his cheek against hers and purring, and she has signed up for a half marathon in Spring (well, you can imagine my thoughts on this): and also, what is worse - Larry, I can barely even say this - a pole fitness course in Chesterfield. I actually consider this to be bringing the Embassy into disrepute. Second Employee is a good twenty years too old to be setting off down the A6 to clamber up a pole in shorts. In fact, if Second Employee manages to *find* her shorts to start with she will already have exceeded my *most optimistic* expectations. Esso and I have discussed this, and we wondered if, given the Bad Corvids situation, there could perhaps be another lockdown: a very, very focused one which only applies to Second Employee and leaves everyone else alone? We think this would be for the best. Thank you, Larry - we will try very hard to hold the fort here while we await your instructions!

December 2021

Larry, the Catinet, and employees. This is Esso, Ambassador to the High Peak, taking a moment (while Second Employee is rushing round in a panic, and First Employee is yet again considering whether he should go with the Elizabeth David recipe for the goose tomorrow even though NO-ONE LIKES GOOSE) to wish you all a happy Christy-Maus, Christmas, or Yule, or whatever you call it in your particular dialect. Ghost and I hope you have a lovely time, and Second Employee says to tell you she'll 'see you all on the other side'. Honestly, Second Employee, it's not an ordeal to get through. Now get those mince pies in the oven, get that candelabra lit, your mother and father will be here in twenty minutes, and we have to put on a decent show here at the Embassy!

December 2021

Larry and the Catinet; Esso here, Ambassador to the High Peak, with FINALLY some good news to report. First Employee has got a disease! Now, Ghost was supposed to be keeping on top of this situation, and she has been saying all along it was something to do with Corvids, and I can see why she thought that, because the Jackdaws here are very difficult. Really very difficult. But it is apparently not about the Naughty Jackdaws. It is a disease. And the good news is, it means Second Employee can't go out until she has got something called a 'negative PCR test'. First Employee doesn't seem to want to go out, because he keeps sneezing for some reason or other, and Second Employee says there is 'not a chance in hell' that his PCR test will be negative. We think he should rest for a bit, anyway. But Ghost and I have been keeping a very, very close eye on Second Employee, because we were worried over Christmas that she was going down an *unfortunate path*.

Larry, we disapproved very strongly of some of the presents she received: you won't believe this - *we* barely could - but someone gave her some more dungarees, even worse than the ones she has already; and her brother gave her a painting, when we have got more than enough pictures in this house. More than enough. Also, Second Employee announced over Christmas lunch that it was 'actually quite difficult having cats when you were an introvert, and in the New Year she was going to become a Quaker'. Well, we can't have Second Employee becoming a Quaker, because she is already a Pagan, and that causes us enough trouble: we won't mention the Solstice Ritual, which began with her burning a piece of paper in a candle flame and ended in the garden with Ghost having to supervise her trying to put out a fire in a biscuit tin.

What is more, Second Employee failed to be an appropriate Ambassador for Buxton when she got her PCR test in Bakewell, even though she knows Bakewell is our great rival. First, because she had to drive her and First Employee there in the car First Employee usually drives, she couldn't work out how to wind the windows down; and while the man was trying to pass her a test kit through the window it kept going up and down, and then she set her wipers off by mistake and started laughing quite a lot; which would not have given the impression of professionalism and competence, which is the image we wish to convey. Then, the man asked her where they were from, and they said Buxton, and he said, oh, that's a very remote kind of place, isn't it, at the top of a hill. I wouldn't go there personally. Second Employee *knows* that when conversations like this arise (which they do quite often), she is supposed to emphasise our Opera Festival and good train connections to Manchester! She knows that! And yet she said nothing! Because 'I am always having to defend Buxton but that was such a strange situation he took me by surprise'.

So it is very, very good news that she is going to be spending more time at home. Ghost has really put some time in with her today via three extended stroking sessions and Intermittent Kneading, and I have made sure that she hasn't taken a single step in the kitchen or the sitting room without me matching it. In fact, she's said more than once, please don't trip me up and kill me, Esso, it's me who gives you your biscuits. So, please keep your fingers crossed for us, Larry, that Second Employee's PCR Test Result is Positive, because if we can make sure she isolates with us for a good ten days - or more, if possible - it may be that we can start to turn her round. We haven't given up on her yet!

December 2021

Larry the Catinet, and assorted Employees who I understand are occasionally allowed to read these updates although if it were up to me I would be careful about indulging them in their pretensions. Esso here, Ambassador to the High Peak, and I am sitting with Second Employee, who has asked me to wish you all a 'Happy New Year'. Even for an occasion like this she hasn't put on a nice, ironed t-shirt under her dungarees! Honestly, Larry, I despair, and, even more disappointingly, her PCR test is negative, so she can apparently go out if she keeps testing. She has promised Ghost and I that she won't go far, but might just 'go for a run up the hill', even though we all know that the last time she did this she got lost in a field, then chased by a sheep, and she consequently told everyone she was 'moving back to bloody Cambridge because I'm no good at the country' until she looked up the prices of houses similar to the Embassy but in Cambridge on Rightmove. So you can understand why I am currently giving her the side-eye. Anyway, Happy New Year from me, Ghost, and the Employees! Best wishes from all of us, and we will see you next year!

January 2022

Larry and the Catinet. This is Ghost here, Ambassador to the High Peak, with an update which will be much more informative than Esso's, which are really just gossip. I mean I don't like to discourage him but we all know.

Anyway. Well, Larry, it won't surprise you to learn that Second Employee has got the Disease now, and, typically she has got entirely the wrong attitude to it. She said to First Employee Thank God she had a 'positive lateral flow' because it would be 'her luck to get a cold, and then get Covid when she'd recovered and have to stay in for another 10 days'. Then she sat on the sofa with a box of tissues and a box of chocolates and emailed everyone and cancelled everything. Well, Larry, Second Employee's mother was FURIOUS because her boiler isn't pressurising properly and she and Second Employee's father wanted to come and stay for a fortnight until it was sorted out, and now they can't. And Second Employee has no proper sense of social duty, because she just said, oh well, there we are. Obviously, Larry, we were unimpressed with her terrible attitude - especially since she didn't even pretend to be disappointed that First Employee also had to cancel an opera they were going to - so Esso went and had a long conversation with Grey Next Door Cat, who told us that we have got the Disease entirely wrong and actually it can be very serious. It is not just sneezing and chocolate and making First Employee watch the Great Pottery Throw Down, and Second Employee has got to make sure she doesn't go into hospital so she isn't a lot of trouble and a Burden On Society. First Employee is much better now - Esso says he has started looking at his spreadsheets again and saying there is no money for a veg box, so he must be feeling well - but it would be just like Second Employee to become a burden on society! And that would reflect very badly on us!

I wish I had finished teaching Second Employee to speak Cat, Larry, because I have not been able to explain to her properly that she has to try not be too ill. Since she got her Positive Lateral Flow I've spent most of my time staring at her to make sure she doesn't deteriorate. Sometimes I have to pop outside to use the facilities or to keep an eye on Graham next door, but when I come back in I make sure to rush and find her immediately, and squeak very loudly, to make sure she hasn't collapsed while I've been out. Earlier she went right up to the top floor to poke about in her wool collection, which I thought was very strenuous in the circumstances, so I chased her and made her sit and stroke me for a good 20 minutes to make sure her breathing was steady. Then I stopped on every step in front of her when she tried to walk back down. Then when she got to the ground floor, Esso took over, and wove all around her legs and head butted her to stop her rushing about. She said, look, are you two trying to trip me up and kill me while I'm weak, but we weren't, Larry! We are trying to keep her alive!

Grey Next Door Cat said to Esso that employees come and go anyway and it's best to not get attached, and someone else would give us our Royal Canin Biscuits and it would be ok; and that anyway we should have covered this eventuality in the 2022 High Peak Embassy Risk Register (note to self: tell Esso to write a 2022 High Peak Embassy Risk Register). But Grey Next Door Cat doesn't understand that Second Employee strokes my cheeks and tells me I am a fabulous cat, and says, look at you, Ghostycat, you're the prettiest cat in the whole of the High Peak. I'm not attached. Obviously. But it remains the case that those are necessary and important Employee functions, and who knows if other employees would be as diligent. So I am determined to keep Second Employee alive until our next update, even if it involves round-the-clock kneading, constant squeaking, or grabbing her leg at surprising moments from under the sofa to keep her alert. I know you'll be impressed with my dedication, Larry, and when things quieten down I'd like us to revisit that discussion about my transfer to Derbyshire Dales!

January 2022

Larry. Ghost, Very Distinguished Ambassador to the High Peak here with my very careful and considered update. Well, I have had to have some words with Esso. I am rather cross with him. All he has been doing recently, frankly, has been LOUNGING in front of the fire. He says we have all had a very busy time over the Festival of Cat Toys Tied To A Tree, and then trying to keep the Employees alive when they selfishly managed to catch The Disease through scruffing about Down South; and he says that it's important to have a rest while we can. But Larry, I think this is just an excuse. He knows as well as I do that White Back Lane Cat has been prowling round and we need to get out there and renegotiate territory!

Esso says as well that he's doing important work guarding Second Employee's Crochet-Throw-In-Progress, and what if White Back Lane Cat were to break in and try and steal it. But Larry, who is going to steal it? Really? It is horrible. I am making it a New Year Resolution to really work on Second Employee's understanding of Cat, the One True Language, because I have got a list of things to say to her, and the first one is, Second Employee, it is FAR PAST time for you to embrace greige as a concept. Second Employee says she 'cannot cope with you forever popping up out of nowhere, Ghost, and judging me', and yes, Second Employee, I am certainly judging you. In 2022 there will be no pink walls, there will be no ridiculous eBay candelabras, and there will ESPECIALLY be no big bright pictures! Now I have managed to keep you alive, at enormous personal cost - Larry, the following about and squeaking and grabbing and kneading it took, I can't even begin to tell you - we are having a clean slate. We are beginning again. We are having calm, sophistication, neutral colours and above all NO CROCHET in the Embassy, or my name is not Ghostycat, the Softest Cat in Buxton!

January 2022

Larry and the Catinet. Esso here, Ambassador to the High Peak. Well, I have a Special Report and Retrospective today, Larry, because Second Employee has told us - and I think you will find this *astonishing* - that it is three years today since we took up our posts here in the High Peak. Three whole years! And as I lie here in front of the Special Fire, which First Employee lights just for me during the Happy Cold Times, I reflect on the progress we have made since we arrived as slightly smaller but still extremely professional Ambassadors. Ghost and I have perused a photo of our Younger Selves, in which Ghost in particular has an expression of eagerness to begin delivering the High Peak Embassy Stategic Plan. I confess it took me a little longer to adjust, and indeed to believe that anyone had deliberately a built a town with quite so many hills in it. I don't think First Employee still entirely believes it. And yet it is the case!

It was cold when we first got here, too, from the much milder climes of Chesterfield, which is the Last Centre of Known Civilisation before the vast unexplored wilderness of the High Peak. Our first introduction to the Embassy wasn't ideal, because First Employee panicked and dropped our cat carrier; so we both shot out the front bit of it practically on to the A6, and then he scooped us up WILDLY and threw us through the front door shouting to Second Employee 'Oh my God Susie I'm an idiot, I nearly lost the bloody kittens'. Ghost and I retreated tactically to a furry igloo which had thoughtfully been provided, and made the mutual decision never to leave the igloo again (there have been many times since when I wish we had stuck to this resolution): but Second Employee came and lay down on the floor and assured us that there were no Kitten Murderers in the house, and that we could come out and run round and round and round and up the curtains with impunity. Larry, what a three years it has been! The many territory negotiations with Grey Next Door Cat: the Shocking Intrusion of the Unfixed Tabby, where he ate our biscuits SHAMELESSLY while looking Second Employee Right In The Eye, and she had to ring First Employee to ask him what to do (and then completely failed to carry out his helpful advice of 'for God's sake, Susie, just tap him on the bum with the brush and he'll go out'): The unfortunate occasion where Second Employee's father became unaccountably bitten by my teeth, and Second Employee's mother forced the Employees to come back early from faffing about in A Mousehole: The time when Interim Summer Employee told Second Employee she was not firm enough with us and that he would give us our flea spot while she was in Andalucia, and then when she came back told her that Ghost was 'literally able to read his mind and reacted really quite alarmingly' and he never wanted to give us our flea spots ever again: the many happy Festivals of Cat Toys Tied To A Tree: and all the wonderful work we have done bringing Civilisation to the Cats and Employees of the High Peak.

Only one negative remains, Larry: Second Employee is still not performing to standard, and in fact Ghost and I have had to invoke the High Peak Feline Embassy Employee Capability Procedure and put her on special measures. It involves one of us being within six feet of her at all times, and preferably sitting on her and nibbling/ headbutting/ kneading her. It is useful because it has coincided with a drop in temperature, and neither of us wants to go out, and Second Employee is nice and warm for kneading on. So we continue to do our duty, and to at least *try* to bring the light of Culture to the darkness of the High Peak!

January 2022

Larry. This is Ghost, Ambassador to the High Peak, with a very, very serious update. I'm afraid I have to discuss what a MASSIVE HYPOCRITE my brother Esso has been, and how he is QUITE WRONG about me. My feelings really are *extremely* hurt. He took me to one side yesterday and said he had noticed I kept staking Second Employee out so I could knead on her and suck her jumper. You won't believe this, Larry, but he impugned my motives: he said it wasn't helpful to get 'too attached' to the Employees, and that he had told me about it before. Well, as you know, I am no more attached to Second Employee than I am to the free Waitrose magazine lying untidily on the floor (Second Employee is a sucker for a free Waitrose magazine, even though they are surely bad for the environment, and we are probably sacrificing ENTIRE RAINFORESTS just so she can read a few haggis recipes and an interview with Kenneth Branagh). Anyway, I suck on her jumper to glean information about where she's been and what she might have been doing, for example: it combines meditation with information-gathering. For instance, after tonight's extended session I can tell you that she hasn't gone out at all today because it's been too cold, but has spent the afternoon making soup, hummus and Bircher Muesli; even though every time she makes Bircher Muesli she doesn't want to eat it the morning after, and says oh sod it it's too cold I'll have a poached egg. So you see how informative my kneading and sucking is.

And when Esso says she will get the wrong idea and it distracts her from her important Employee work, that is nonsense, because herein lies his terrible hypocrisy! I am going to describe to you a particular scene which unfolded earlier.

Second Employee had been sitting on the sofa downstairs reading for a long time, then looked up, and squealed in shock. Esso had been Lurking and Watching on the Cupboard Near The Window, and was Peeping Out at her from behind the Dodgy Lamp. He says all he was doing was contemplating why all the lamps in our house have got wonky shades, and was it related to me 'bouncing off them when you go a bit mad at three in the morning, Ghost': but clearly Second Employee was very alarmed, and she has a delicate constitution, so it will probably make her (even) less effective for at least the next week. So I think you can see very clearly from my update, Larry, that the one *actually* causing staff problems here is Esso, and if you could let him know that, it would be helpful, and also if you could write me a note to say I can knead and suck on Second Employee whenever I want to without Esso mithering me and saying I am emotionally attached which really is almost beyond ridiculous, that would be helpful too. Thank you Larry, and I am continuing to do lots of very helpful work on Staff Development here until I finally get my transfer to Derbyshire Dales!

February 2022

Larry and the Catinet: This is Esso, Ambassador to the High Peak. I thought I should just do an update to reassure you. Particularly after recent events over here. We're all fine now, so don't worry (well, Second Employee is still bleeding a bit). I'm completely relaxed on my back with my LEGGIES in the air.

Nothing to worry about! Anyway Ghost just had a bit of a mad moment. And she'd been doing so well! She's been out every day intimidating White Back Lane Cat who's been making INROADS, and it's sorted him right out. She comes in every evening with her tail fluffed up just like a bottle cleaner. it's no wonder White Cat is scared, I would be too; but then we had the unfortunate incident.

Ghost was sitting on the wooden chest in the first floor front room, amongst First Employee's ceramic pig collection, nosing at what was going on out the front - the people who live in one of the new houses over the road with Scary Tortoiseshell Cat are having their roof done, and I *personally* wouldn't trust them to make any design choices given what they've done with their raised beds - when she saw Second Employee drive back, park, and come into the house. Well. I've been telling Ghost for a good three years that Second Employee has got her own car. I knew she hadn't been listening, because she was HORRIFIED. That evening, I could tell she was brooding. She said, but Esso, what if she drives away and doesn't come back to do her duty here. Then, this morning, the Employees went out, and Ghost was upset. She said Esso, she's gone, and we'll have to appoint another Employee, and you know how much trouble it is and I can't bear to have to shortlist against core competencies again, I can't bear it Esso. I said, look Ghost, you know they'll come back, they always come back because they know their duty, and besides you know Second Employee likes her sofa. And being close to the fridge and the kettle. But Ghost got herself into a state. And then when they did come back, she leapt on Second Employee and kneaded so vigorously that Second Employee is all scratched and bleeding, which is worrying because she is exactly the kind of Employee to go septic and cause trouble: and I said to Ghost, look at all the effort you put in to keep her alive through Covid, don't kill her with too much love! So Ghost is upset because she says she doesn't love anybody, Second Employee is upset because she's quite scratched up, and First Employee is upset because when he told Second Employee she was 'too soft with that little cat' she told him he was 'victim blaming'; and First Employee says that is ridiculous and no-one can be the victim of a 'tiny, gentle white cat'. Well, that's not quite how I'd describe Ghost, and I don't think that's how the vet, Interim Summer Employee, or Second Employee's mother would describe her either. And White Back Lane Cat certainly wouldn't! So we're all going to have a quiet, calm couple of days and heal our emotional and physical wounds. Ghost is upstairs composing a letter to the DVLA to have Second Employee's driving licence taken away 'because she can't be trusted and is generally quite rubbish', but I really don't think that's fair: don't worry, Larry, I'll talk her out of it, and I really think our next update will be much more cheerful and constructive!

February 2022

Larry and the Catinet, this is Ghost, Ambassador to the High Peak, with very important things to discuss. No wonder I look a little ruffled in this photograph! I think Esso told you yesterday about my SHOCKING DISCOVERY that Second Employee has got her own car and is roaming round the High Peak causing all sorts of trouble. Esso says he's actually been telling me this for three years and I haven't been listening, but that is only because he is always telling me such pointless things that I have to ignore him. Ghost, he says, the Waitrose delivery man told me I was a delightful cat, did you hear him Ghost. Ghost, why have you started eating the biscuits from the pink bowl when we agreed to boycott that one and only eat out of the grey one. Ghost, what did you say to the Poltergeist in the basement, because you've upset him again and he's sulking. So that is Esso's fault for normally talking rubbish and making me not listen when *literally once in a blue moon* he says something useful!

And now he says, well Ghost, what does it matter anyway if Second Employee goes roaming about in her Small Scruffy Blue Car, what harm is it doing. Well, Larry, I think you will appreciate the harm; but just in case you are going to be perverse like Esso I will spell it out. Second Employee is not a bright Employee. She is easily distracted by shiny things. If she realises there is a large TK Maxx in Sheffield, or a Vintage

Emporium in Stockport, she may go wandering off in her car, get confused looking at shelves of lamps in the shape of monkeys or Fat Lava vases OR WORSE, and then forget how to get home to Buxton to do her duty. Then she may try to make a new life in Sheffield or Stockport or wherever, possibly feebly attempting to forage leftover cake, or being fed by kind householders. She may even end up in an Employee Shelter. Because of some ridiculous protocol, we do not have the Employees chipped, so if this happens it will be very difficult for Esso and I to prove ownership; and I'm sure you can appreciate that after the HOURS I have put into training the Employees I am very reluctant to start again from scratch.

I would therefore like to propose *immediate* chipping of all Employees - I am amazed, frankly, that this isn't done anyway as a matter of course - and I would also suggest that it would be better to make them House Employees rather than letting them go out and wander the neighbourhood, where they are at risk of all sorts of things; for example slipping down our back hill when it is icy, which is all the time except for those two weeks in July, or being pecked by a Jackdaw. There is no need for them to go out anyway - the fact that Esso seems to have built up a relationship with the Waitrose delivery man (who only thinks Esso is delightful because he hasn't met me!) proves that they have got a means of getting food. I have written to the DVLA in any case, Larry, requesting withdrawal of Second Employee's driving licence on the grounds of her general ineptitude, and I await your instructions regarding new Chipping and Confining To Houses legislation. I think it is time, Larry, that these anarchic elements in the High Peak Embassy Strategic Plan 2022-2023 were brought properly under control!

February 2022

Larry and the Catinet, Ghost here, Ambassador to the High Peak with my very useful, objective, and well-observed report. Well, those naughty Jackdaws have been very difficult recently. They've been shouting at me! When I was under my special radiator! 'Ghostycat, Ghostycat, we can see you Ghostycat, we're going to come in and peck you!' they were shouting! Well of course they can't come in and peck Ambassadors, but it's very disturbing to have to listen to that rude kind of talk all the same. Anyway, Esso did some very good work last night negotiating with them - he said they managed to come to a mutual understanding about courtesy and boundaries - and then he came in to check on the Employees, because if we take our eyes off them for too long something always goes wrong. He said when he came into the sitting room, though, it was nice and warm, and so he only actually got as far as the Big Leafy Plant before he flopped right over and closed his eyes just for a moment. He woke up an hour later, with his mouth open and all his LEGGIES in the air at different but equally impressive angles, to find the Employees standing over him; and Second

Employee said, I don't know how anyone can hurt them, do you? And they both looked sad.

Esso says she meant that sometimes Employees are not kind to Ambassadors, and I have not got to think about it and not to worry my small, very silky head, and to go back to worrying about the Jackdaws. But I personally am wondering whether Second Employee was actually referring to the time last year when Esso and I had to hurt quite a large number of mice, in fact we had to sacrifice them all on the Employees' bed to make them come back from Andalucia where they had not got proper permission to go anyway. There was quite a lot of blood, if I'm honest. Interim Summer Employee was not supposed to tell them about any of it. He was supposed to just wash the duvet and not mention it. So if I find he has ratted us out to Second Employee I will consider what my next steps should be, because there are things I know about Interim Summer Employee that I think he would also not like passed on, and also if I felt very strongly I could always tell the Jackdaws that he was rude about them, even though that is not strictly true. In fact, he thinks the Jackdaws are 'amazing birds', which they most certainly are not. They are actually *dreadfully common things*. Anyway, Larry, could you pass a few laws please, firstly to stop Interim Summer Employee from telling the Employees my secrets, and also to stop Second Employee from standing over Esso and making gnomic utterances, because the one useful thing about Second Employee is that she is completely transparent and predictable, so if she is going to become Enigmatic it will cause us no end of trouble. Thank you Larry, and I hope you're glad to see how well we're continuing to deliver the High Peak Embassy Strategic Plan 2002-2023!

February 2022

Larry and the Catinet; it's Esso here, Ambassador to the High Peak, with my important report. Oh God, Larry, it's been a difficult couple of days. Ghost is FURIOUS. She says she won't do the report today and I've got to do it 'because if I start saying anything at all I'll say too much, Esso'. Well, Larry, the upshot of it all is, Second Employee wandered back yesterday afternoon and announced that she's now a Ceramicist, and she's 'going to be doing some handbuilding on the second floor'. As I'm sure you can imagine: Ghost took it badly. Ghost says she's put up with the pink dining room, the wool everywhere ('and putting you near that amount of wool is like putting Dracula in a bloodbank, Esso, how anyone thinks I can be expected to control this situation *I do not know!*') and the terrible bright pictures from all of the Employees' artist friends (I must say, I do agree with Ghost here that we can't really understand why the Employees can't make a few friends who enjoy something useful, like gardening, or rewiring old houses), but she absolutely *will not* put up with wobbly vases on all the surfaces and 'it's only a matter of time, Esso, before she replaces our food bowls with awful wonky things with a smudgy paw-print in some terrible amateur-looking underglaze'.

To be honest with you, Larry, I think Ghost feels personally betrayed, because she helped Second Employee put the new Ceramic Handbuilding table up without realising what it was for; and without Ghost, Second Employee would have had to sniff every single bolt individually herself. Anyway, Ghost will not be swayed, and she says we need to get rid of Second Employee immediately and she's written an updated job description for her replacement. I've reproduced it here in full for you, Larry.

Job Description for Second Employee Mark 2: First Draft, for discussion with Catinet.
Author: Ghost

1/ Must be softly spoken, and move slowly like Second Employee. We understand this is because Second Employee has very low Iron in her blood, so someone at a similar stage of anaemia would be ideal.
2/ Must be willing to come up to second floor on command (squeak) for stroking and kneading and not complain if this becomes extended or is repeated frequently. Must feel exactly the same to knead as Second Employee does, and wear the same jumper. We feel it's unlikely to be an expensive one.

3/ Must stroke my whiskers back whenever we meet on the stairs, and tell me I am the prettiest, best, and softest cat in the whole of the High Peak.

4/ Must allow/ encourage entry of Ambassadors into the Exciting Spice Cupboard during pre-bed tidy of kitchen for appropriate auditing.

5/ Must smell exactly the same as Second Employee except for that horrible hand cream, and we do not care if Second Employee thinks she has developed contact dermatitis, that is her own fault for going about touching clay.

6/ Must have no interest at all in any of the following: Becoming a Ceramicist: Wool: Painting Dining Room Pink: Putting Flea Medication on the necks of Ambassadors.

Now, Larry, I have pointed out to Ghost that the only person who can meet points 1-5 is actually Second Employee; and that perhaps she, Ghost, needs to be a bit less controlling, and accept Second Employee as a Flawed Human Being with interests Ghost doesn't approve of. This has gone down as I expected. Could I request, Larry, that you just ignore any missives from Ghost for the next few days - any requests for transfers, sackings, or new legislation specifically relating to underglaze - and I'll try and calm the situation down here. Hopefully, Larry, soon we can get back to building on my earlier success with the Jackdaws - and also I'm rather looking forward to Second Employee bringing some clay back here - if it's as much fun as her wool I'm going to have a good time!

February 2022

Larry, it's Ghost here, Ambassador to the High Peak, with my very useful and rather intellectual update. Well, Larry, I was just about to recruit a new, improved Second Employee - Esso told me he gave you my draft Job Description, and you thought it was excellent - but then we had very dramatic weather: so I've decided to put things on hold for a moment until the weather settles down, which Esso says is normally for at least a week in July. Or even two weeks. So we're going to time our recruitment for then. In the meantime I've been explaining to Second Employee that she shouldn't go out when it is very windy, because she is the type of Employee who can't be trusted not to get herself squashed under a falling tree or something like that. Alas, my advice was in vain, because she went out yesterday afternoon to 'throw a pot on a wheel' (we have no idea what this involves, Larry, but we do apologise if she's causing criminal damage to cars) and came back looking exactly like a drowned rat, and swearing: saying, it has rained for four weeks solidly and she has never bloody known anything like it and she will bloody move and that will bloody show everyone. Then, though, Larry, First Employee said a SHOCKING thing, which Esso and I have been thinking about and trying to analyse. He said - and I'm quoting this verbatim - 'look, darling, why don't we just move to Spain' and then he looked at his phone and said 'it's going to be 21 degrees in Andalucia all next week. We could be settled at the house in a month or so'. And Second Employee looked at him and said 'are you volunteering to spend the *rest of your life* fiddling about with Ghost's ears then?' and he said - imagine this, Larry! - 'yes, I'll put sun cream on Ghost's ears every thirty minutes all day every day. But you know she'll love it. We'll see her wandering through the village at the head of a family of wild boars and a couple of mountain goats, organising them. She'll be in her element'. What does this mean, Larry? Esso says there are places in the world even wilder and higher up than the High Peak, and with creatures more insubordinate than Jackdaws: and not to engage with First Employee, because no-one is going anywhere until Second Employee looks us right in the eyes and tells us that she's willing to drive in a car with us singing the Ballad of The Disgruntled Kitten for two and a half thousand kilometres, and to share a cabin with us for twenty-four hours on the Southampton-Bilbao ferry.

But I think, perhaps there are some wild boars and mountain goats somewhere who do need organising, and perhaps I'm the Ambassador to do it. [Note from Esso: oh, if only Ghost had never gone down this road which was ill-starred!] I don't know what this is about cream on my ears, and obviously I'm not having that at all. But I don't always listen to Esso anyway, because all he's been doing recently has been nudging his head against Second Employee and purring and patting her with his paw, and when I say to him, enough of this, Esso, you've got an image to keep up, he says he won't be caught in the trap of Toxic Masculinity and if he wants to show affection he will do! Larry, there is no wonder we have such insubordination from the Employees if Esso is going to be going about showing them affection! Nothing could be worse, for Second Employee in particular. Don't worry, though, I'm taking control of this situation. I'm off out now to deal with Black and White Pink Collar Cat who's been trying to take control of our back garden, and later Esso and I will be having strong words. I'll keep appropriate professional boundaries in this Embassy if it's the last thing I do!

February 2022

Larry. This is Ghost here, Ambassador to the High Peak, with a SERIOUS CONCERN. Larry, the more Esso and I think about what First Employee said about putting 'sun cream' on my ears every thirty minutes in case of both the employees taking complete leave of their senses and relocating us all to Andalucia as a ridiculous overreaction to a tiny bit of rain, the more we feel I am being picked on. As Esso says, there is no material difference between us, so why should I be targeted? We are even exactly the same colour - both black and white! (I appreciate there are very, very small differences in how it is distributed, but this is hardly significant, surely?!). I'm not suggesting the Employees are acting maliciously, as they are both good-natured, if incompetent: but this seems very strange. Could you try to investigate, Larry? I don't want 'sun cream' on my ears in my future if this is, as seems clear, some strange, unjustified idea Second Employee has got into her head, similar to when she decided she was going to grow all her own vegetables and has not yet managed to sprout a single potato, despite Esso kicking them off the window sill and round the kitchen daily. Many thanks, Larry, and we will await clarification on this matter!

Chapter 5

Spring 2022 is sprung, the grass is riz, and we all know where the birdies is

March 2022

Larry and the Catinet. Ghost here, Ambassador to the High Peak, with my update. Larry, I shall ask you the question I was asking Second Employee earlier, though being met with defensiveness and obfuscation: what induction did the Employees receive? Because Esso and I are wondering if they have really been given the best chance to act effectively in their roles. The other night, First Employee had gone out to sing with other people with his very loud voice, and Second Employee and I were sitting on the sofa with a cup of tea watching Victoria Wood singing a song about Doing It on youTube, when we noticed there was water running down the wall behind the Big Lamp which the movers broke when the Employees set up the Embassy and Second Employee cried and said it was 'Early Habitat' and First Employee mended it so it really only wobbles a bit.

Well, there is always water running down somewhere it shouldn't be in this house, so Second Employee set off to the floor above with her torch, poking at floorboards and saying, it must be a leaky radiator, Ghost! Don't worry! It's not like when we put that nail through the waste pipe and had to call the Emergency Plumber! Anyway: I suddenly had the realisation: how much time do the Employees spend wandering about pointlessly with a torch from floor to floor, looking bewildered? Poking at boilers and leaks, or trying to fix bits of the house that have dropped off? So far First Employee has fixed the towel rail in the first floor toilet four times, and the curtain pole in the second floor bedroom twice; and James the electrician has mended the first floor bathroom light three times and still it isn't working because Second Employee hasn't managed to get the sealant sealed properly in the Second Floor Shower and it keeps leaking through the floorboards and rusting the switch. Which is probably dangerous, Larry, if anyone sensible thought about it carefully.

It just makes Esso and I feel that they don't properly understand the maintenance necessary for a tall, thin, old house, which Second Employee says is 'like something from Gormenghast' (this means nothing to me, Larry, but may to you). Have they perhaps never been taught? Esso says another thing they don't seem to understand is when diplomatic protocols should be relaxed. Second Employee's parents stayed here this weekend, and, despite Esso scratching very loudly at the door of their bedroom at 5am, Second Employee's mother refused to let him in! Esso is very annoyed, because obviously everyone knows that the protocol states that for guests who need a higher degree of etiquette - for example if

Second Employee managed to let the room out on Airbnb like she keeps threatening, although as soon as anyone asked her about local attractions it would reveal that the only walk she knows is from the house to the cake shop and she could not find her way up Mam Tor if her life depended on it - then Ambassadors don't share the room; but when family stay, like Second Employee's parents or Interim Summer Employee, Esso sleeps with them!

Esso says he has an excellent arrangement with Interim Summer Employee, whereby Esso comes in at dawn, jumps right on top of him, and bites him if he wakes up or turns over: and the only time Interim Summer Employee ever complained was when Esso bit him hard, right on his new tattoo. And we don't think Second Employee's mother has any new tattoos, so there is *literally* no reason why she shouldn't have let Esso in, and Second Employee should have known enough to advise her of appropriate behaviour. But we want to move forwards with the Employees and their inadequacies, Larry: if you could send me details of the induction programme they've undergone so far, Esso and I will look at it and try to plug any gaps. Esso and I think that will save on DISGRUNTLEMENTS and RESENTMENTS and BLAMINGS going forward!

March 2022

Larry, this is Esso, Ambassador to the High Peak, with my update. Larry, I have shocked Ghost to the CORE. I feel you may receive a communication from her. But, the world is different these days, and I feel I am actually a PIONEER of emotional literacy and communication in the Cat Diplomatic Service. I shall explain what has transpired. Ghost approached me yesterday and said, OK Esso, I think we should make a plan for those two weeks in July when it stops raining and we are going to recruit a new, improved version of Second Employee, because I am wondering if we should put the advert just in the Buxton Advertiser or if we should widen it out to Leek as well. Well, I said, firstly I think there is no point advertising it to anybody in Leek because the road over the Cat and Fiddle is terrible. So we should just advertise it in Buxton. Actually perhaps also London, Paris and Milan, because then they could get the train: and apparently you can get to Buxton if you change at Stockport and so we are not reliant on First Employee picking people up from Chesterfield Station in his Small Grey Peugeot any more. But, more importantly, Ghost, we are actually not going to advertise at all, because, I love Second Employee and I don't want her to leave.

Well, Ghost looked at me *completely gone out*, as they say up here, but I continued. I love Second Employee, I said, and we have a special relationship which I *will not* transfer to whatever greige-painting coldly efficient robot you want to inflict on us, Ghost. Yes, now I have renounced my toxic masculinity and become more in touch with my emotions, I am happy to say that Second Employee and I are special friends: I lay my cheek against hers and purr, and bite her feet to motivate her to get going in the mornings: while she dries me with a teatowel when I've been out in the rain, and calls me Mr Cuddles. We are very happy together. And just because she only calls you Mrs Nosy Noser, Ghost, it is perhaps time to recognise that not only are you motivated by jealousy, but also that it is a very accurate name: because honestly you can hear Second Employee doing something you disapprove of when she is in the basement and you are three floors up under your radiator, and you are right down there JUDGING within ten seconds every time. So, Ghost, I said, there will be no recruitment procedure, and if you are unhappy you will just have to think of a way to not be unhappy, because anyway if we recruit a new Second Employee you will feel that the way she loads the dishwasher is inefficient or something equally ridiculous and we will be back to square one.

So Larry, I would just request that when Ghost inevitably contacts you within the next few days asking for me to be dismissed and/ or imprisoned, do not act on anything quickly. I think these things needed to be said, and I am hopeful that in a few days she and I will be able to re-establish our previous constructive relationship! Yours, Esso.

Larry - Ghost here - Larry, Esso says Second Employee doesn't love me even a tiny, tiny bit. Larry, what shall I do?!

March 2022

Larry and the Catinet, Ghost here with my Important Update. Well, Larry, after Esso's revelation that he and Second Employee had struck up a special relationship which did not include me, and without it having been run past me for my approval, I went to the First Floor Landing to sit watching the Portal. The Portal is a mysterious door in between the First Floor and the Ground Floor, which folds in on itself, and out of it sometimes strange people come. It must be a Portal to other realities. Esso says it is not a Portal to other realities and actually it is just a toilet, and all that has happened is that Second Employee once snuck guests into the house 'in that five minutes a day when you're actually asleep and not nosing round, Ghost' and I caught one of them coming out of it later and didn't understand where they'd come from so have worried ever since. And he says the door folds in on itself mysteriously 'because there wasn't room for a normal door, Ghost, because someone at some stage has just stuck that toilet there without a proper plan and bodged it, like everything else in this house'. Obviously this is nonsense, and shows that Esso has no understanding of either Teleportation or the Supernatural. So I thought it was a good idea to keep an eye on The Portal just in case anything else disturbing happened.

First Employee went in, came out again, saw me, jumped, and said hello Ghostycat what are you doing there lurking? Then he went downstairs and said to Second Employee, Susie, Ghost is being creepy on the stairs and watching me with the Cold Eyes of Judgement. So Second Employee came up and took a photo of me because she said I was being a Fabulously Dramatic Cat, and then she stroked my cheeks and said I was the most precious, most special cat in the whole world and she loved me very much. So I stood up, said BRRRRRRRPPPP, and came to headbutt Second Employee and lick her with my extremely rough tongue, because she is a bit of a scruff and she needs regular grooming by me to look even halfway decent. I don't know why Esso thinks he has the special relationship with Second Employee when actually she and I have been best friends since I was a little kitten in temporarily difficult circumstances. I have decided, entirely independently of Esso and his renunciation of toxic masculinity, not to recruit a new Second Employee: because recruitment is very hard work, and what if we got someone who seemed perfect and had a portfolio of things she had painted greige and then as soon as she was in post did something unforgivable, like changing our biscuits to a different brand. And also, as Esso says, not everyone would be as diligent as Second Employee at monitoring the temperature every single night from October to

April so she can tape the cat flap up with masking tape if it is forecast to go below freezing overnight, because once the catflap froze solid with Esso on the wrong side of it, and he was terribly inconvenienced until everyone got up and fetched him in. So I am going to say to Esso we must stop all this nonsense and get on with the job in hand. White Back Lane Cat is being so difficult that even First Employee noticed him earlier today, and I have got to help Second Employee with her gardening, because she has managed to sprout a chive seed and now thinks she is Charlie Dimmock. We are busy Ambassadors, and there is no time for this ridiculous and emotionally incontinent talk about love!

March 2022

Larry and the Catinet, Esso here, Ambassador to the High Peak, with my update. Larry, First Employee has been causing us concern by saying a number of Ridiculous Things recently. Firstly, he and Second Employee were discussing the fact that Second Employee had found a tuft of grey fur under the dining table and whether it meant there had been an Incursion by Grey Next Door Cat (Yes there had! But not to worry, Ghost made the point very firmly about where our territory begins by peeing in the purple glass vase on the windowsill. She is very dedicated. Once she marked our territory by peeing in the toaster. That certainly showed Grey Cat!) and Second Employee said, isn't it odd how there are no coloured cats on our street at all. All the cats are either black, white, grey, or a combination thereof. We are the Street of The Monochrome Cats. And First Employee said, well, that's probably because we're in a bit of a dodgy area. Perhaps no-one can afford a ginger one. Well, First Employee is wrong about the Embassy being in a 'slightly dodgy area', whatever he means by that. The people here are very friendly. The other day Second Employee's parents came to visit, and somehow, just at the point when Second Employee's Mother pressed the doorbell, Second Employee had decided to go into the basement and whip some cream for a rhubarb fool with her electric mixer and couldn't hear it. So the Employee Parents had to hang about outside the front of the house for a few minutes, and some very friendly men came and chatted to them, who were pouring vodka into their cans of Special Brew. And they offered some to Second Employee's Mother! And she must have been impressed, because she didn't stop talking about it all day. So what First Employee said is nonsense, and especially about ginger cats being more expensive when surely if there was any trade in cats, which of course there isn't, it would be cats who look like me and Ghost and especially me who am like a Velvety Night Sky who would fetch almost impossibly high prices!

Then he said another ridiculous thing. He was talking about our Hydrangea in the front garden and saying it looked scruffy, and Second Employee said, that is what Hydrangeas look like, you just don't like uncontrollable green things and Verdant Life. And

First Employee said, yes this is true actually, when my first wife left me I had all the garden concreted over and it was great. Larry, this has worried Ghost. She said to me, is Second Employee not First Employee's first wife? How does that work? And I had to say to Ghost, Ghost, I'm pretty sure she's not even his second. And now Ghost is confused about how Employees have the energy to have complicated personal lives when our experience is that they spend a lot of time on sofas, saying, whose turn is it to get the coffee, and have we got any more creme eggs. We are basing this primarily on our careful and prolonged observation of Second Employee. I have said to Ghost, it is better not to fret about these things, and to get as much rest as possible, as I am doing now. In fact, we both need to be well-rested in case Ghost needs to pee on the toaster again tonight, because it takes a surprising amount of emotional energy!

March 2022

Larry and the Catinet. This is Ghost, Ambassador to the High Peak, checking in briefly. I'm keeping a very close eye on Second Employee this morning. She's doing something called a 'bank reconciliation' on her laptop for that silly little hobby job Esso and I allow her to have, and I really don't think she's going to be doing her end-of-year journals correctly later based on my past experience of Second Employee and Quickbooks. A very slapdash approach to expenses allocation, that's all I'll say. Also, she thinks it's amusing that I'm sitting under a drawing of a disapproving cat which her brother did for her years ago 'before she got an even more disapproving cat of her own'. Well, this shows once again Second Employee's lack of understanding of who owns whom in this household. Never mind. We continue to work on her! (Also, I'm appalled by how wonky those pictures are, Larry. Honestly, I don't think there is a straight picture in the entirety of this house. I will make sure to add that to her workplan!)

March 2022

Larry, Esso here, Ambassador to the High Peak, with my update. Larry, Second Employee has, entirely accidentally, brought up an interesting issue which we may need to think about. Because Ghost and I took our collective eye off her for a single moment a few weeks ago, she decided to start going to Pole Fitness Classes in Chesterfield. We are unsure how she reconciles this with her Radical Feminism, but somehow she has managed it, so off she goes once a week to spin feebly round a pole and say to everyone, I used to be much better at this. Yes, Second Employee, two stones ago. [Note from Esso: now three]. Then she comes back and eats her weight in CAKE because she needs the energy.

Anyway this brings me to my point, Larry. Second Employee combines her pole fitness with a visit to her parents, because somehow they have managed to live almost next door to a pole studio even though if you had ever met Second Employee's mother you would agree with me that it is an unlikely combination. So, Second Employee tells us she walked in to her parents' house, and her brother was sitting at the table and said, hello Susie, mum tells me you've taken up Lap Dancing. Now, we understand this is a different sport, but Second Employee's mother had APPARENTLY become simply confused and not passive-aggressive at all, and had 'told all our relations and neighbours'. Second Employee's brother said he had corrected her but had initially 'wondered if that was going to be your plan to heat that big mad old house you live in'.

Ghost says this must be a joke, although we don't really get it; and clearly Second Employee has brought the Embassy into disrepute again but 'if you're going to insist on being emotionally aware and loving people, Esso, this is the kind of thing it leads to'. Anyway, on discussion with Grey Next Door Cat and very careful observation of First Employee and his spreadsheets, we have uncovered a Very Serious Issue, which is that the price of energy is going up astronomically, and First Employee has had to talk about Cutting Down Seriously. Second Employee says they could economise by not going to see any 'live opera link-ups' at the cinema in Altrincham, and they could start straight away by *in particular* not going to see the extremely boring one in a fortnight which is four hours long, and that the thing they categorically should not economise on is the buying of dodgy 70s things from eBay because one day her collection of Denby Arabesque might be worth some money. [Note from Esso: it will not.] Hopefully, Larry, this will be enough.

But Larry, I have a secret, terrible fear which I dare not communicate to Ghost. Ghost says, whatever happens, she likes a nice warm house, and will make it clear to the Employees that her Special Radiator has to be kept on at all appropriate times and there is to be no decline in living standards. But Larry: what if this is not possible?! What if Second Employee's economies, stringent though they are, are not enough? The Employees may then be in a situation where they are under continual pressure from Ghost to provide something they simply cannot: and in that case, they may have to consider something currently quite unthinkable. Larry, I can barely bring myself to say it... but what if Second Employee uses some of her leftover wool and knits Ghost a jumper?! And says, there you are, Ghost, you don't need your radiator after all, that will keep you warm? Larry, when I think of what Ghost's reaction to this would be, I shudder. I will keep this fear to myself for the moment and await further advice from the Catinet!

March 2022

Larry and the Catinet, Esso here, Ambassador to the High Peak, checking in with my update. Larry, Spring has come even to the High Peak; I have been looking through the top floor landing window at the lovely sunshine. Second Employee would like me to tell you she runs up the hills we have been looking at through that window sometimes; but Larry, Second Employee is being slightly economical with the truth here in her desire to appear more like an Athlete than like someone who Ghost saw eating three creme eggs in a row earlier today: the truth is, I'm afraid, that she recently got lost on one of those hills, a sheep 'looked at her quite aggressively', and she has stuck to roads ever since where she can monitor which houses are up for sale, and who has bought curtains of which she disapproves. I do not wish to be unkind in saying this: but Strict Veracity is of the utmost importance in my reports.

Well, Larry, I'm afraid Ghost has caused a bit of a diplomatic incident. Second Employee has for a long time been labouring under the belief that Ghost and I never venture to the front of the Embassy, where she doesn't want us to go because it is too busy: this belief is based almost solely on the fact that the jitty at the end of our row is very steep and dangerous and a MASSIVE FAFF for Second Employee to walk up. There was once an incident involving some Ikea Delivery Men and a sofa which had to be brought down the side so it could go in the dining room in the basement. Unfortunately First Employee, who is good at organising people to get furniture into places, and who managed to get a Baby Grand Piano in though our narrow hallway and a Super Kingsize Bed up a spiral staircase in the house in Spain even though the delivery man looked him right in the eye and said 'Es Imposible!', was not there; and Second Employee, who is sensitive, said that the older delivery man in particular looked as if he had 'passed through the Valley of the Shadow Of Death' when he had hauled the sofa down the passage. Because it almost defeated two reluctant, slightly out-of-shape men with a heavy sofa (who were 'pleased our next delivery's in Stockport, love, where it's flat'), she thinks that Ghost, who is lithe and young and lively, does not go up it. This is untrue: but we have been operating on a don't ask-don't tell basis.

Unfortunately, the Employees finally ventured into the front garden to prune the overgrown hydrangea bush, and Ghost just could not stop herself from interfering. She took one look at First Employee wandering off with his secateurs and said, Esso, that man has got no concept of pruning to above a bud and he will kill that hydrangea as soon as look at it: as a result, Second Employee was weeding in the front when she looked up to find Ghost monitoring her accusingly from behind Graham next door's trellis. Second Employee screamed, chased her inside, grabbed her and imprisoned her with me in the sitting room. Larry, Ghost says it was the longest afternoon of her life: she was forced to watch through the window as First Employee 'hacked at that rose willy-nilly' and said unhelpful things like 'why don't we just pave all of this and put the cars on'. Ghost banged on the window with her paw, shouted to Second Employee, and eventually stood on her hind legs and LICKED all the way down the window in her fury: but Second Employee was resolute, and Ghost had to watch, impotently, while First Employee 'butchered that Hydrangea, Esso. He has got the sensitivity of a donkey'. I do not feel that Ghost properly appreciates that she has revealed something that should not be revealed: Second Employee is now watching us both very carefully. It is very inconvenient, Larry, because I would not put it past her to restrict our movements, and Ghost in particular Will Not Be Trammelled. I shall keep you in touch with developments, but I am hopeful I will soon be able to finesse the situation!

[Note from Esso: soon after we moved to the Embassy, the Employees wanted to go out of the front door in the early evening to collect fish and chips. Ghost also wanted to go out the front door, which leads almost directly onto the A6, at exactly the same point of the evening; and so she went out with them. Second Employee screamed, grabbed her, kissed the top of her head, and stuffed her back in the house: the Employees went out, and returned fifteen minutes later with CHIPS to find Ghost sitting looking rather pointed on the front doorstep. They unlocked the door. She walked in with them, silently. Ghost says she was making the point that she cannot be trammelled. It has been effective.]

April 2022

Larry and the Catinet: Esso here, Ambassador to the High Peak, with my update. Larry, Second Employee and I have been reading a book together, about Older People who solve murders. Second Employee's mother has made her read it 'to check if it's any less confusing than his first one before I expend any energy on it, Susie'. This explains the half-price sticker which you can see at the top, because Second Employee's Mother has not paid full price for anything since 1972, when she splashed out the full amount for the wool for an Aran Cardigan which turned out beautifully, albeit with one arm longer than the other, but to her eternal CHAGRIN was then stolen from the back seat of her Mini Cooper. So that certainly taught Second Employee's Mother a lesson, which she Learnt Well.

Larry, things are uneventful here: Ghost has been very industriously peeing on the Large Glass Downstairs Windowsill Vase to show new Black and White Interloper Cat what's what: the weather has very much taken a turn for the worse and we are worried about our seed potatoes which, I have to tell you, were very inadequately chitted to start with: and on Tuesday Second Employee decided to overthrow capitalism. Ghost is a little unhappy about this. She says overthrowing capitalism is all very well and good, and she doesn't mind foraging for her own wild food e.g. voles occasionally, but basically she likes central heating and biscuits on demand. So far, Larry, Second Employee's overthrowing of capitalism seems to consist of making her own soap, which means there is yet another thing in our house which smells of patchouli, and working out cycle routes to the silly little job in the next town which we allow her to do, even though they all involve at least three hills and at least one of them involves a Deep Ravine. And besides, the last time Second Employee rode a bicycle she 'just toppled over randomly', and she surely will have to face reality at some point and accept she is just not up to it.

I have discussed the matter extensively with Grey Next Door Cat, who says not to worry, because Second Employee has no more chance of overthrowing capitalism than she does of getting to the finish line of the Buxton Half Marathon. [Note from Esso: this remains true.] Or indeed to the start line of the Buxton Half Marathon. [Additional note from Esso: this also remains true.] But I am keeping a close eye on the situation, Larry, because obviously we cannot have dangerous sedition in the Employees, and I would be very sad if we had to have Second Employee taken out by the Feline Secret Services. Ghost says so would she, on balance: she was worried her attempts to repel Black and White Interloper Cat were not being appreciated, but that last time Second Employee cleaned up the vase and the windowsill she picked Ghost up, kissed her head, and said, look at you, aren't you the cleverest cat in the whole area, keeping us all safe like this. So now Ghost feels validated, and intends to continue her excellent work, although it will probably mean upping her fluid intake significantly. Second Employee is not a clever Employee, Larry, but we still find her cheering to have around. So we will continue to keep a close eye on the moral development of the Employees, and ensure they are not exposed to dangerous political ideas!

April 2022

Larry, Ghost here, Ambassador to the High Peak, with my update. Second Employee took a photograph of me in the cold light of dawn, in which she says I look like 'the Head of the High Peak Cat Mafia'; which is very rude, Larry, because as you know, everything I do is to uphold Diplomacy, Gracious Living, and the Rule of Law. Besides, I was very tired after a challenging night, and I was also pondering why Second Employee is not capable of ironing a duvet cover.

Something happened recently which I need your advice about, Larry, because I really feel Second Employee may have overstepped her role. It was about 10:30pm. I had left Esso and the Employees to continue their binge watching of Death in Paradise (how they have not even questioned how there could possibly be the same lizard over 3 different detectives so far I *do not know*). Anyway, I was walking up our Side Jitty, and I met Black and White Interloper Cat, sitting there, bold as brass. Hello, Ghost, he said. I understand your Employees are having a loft ladder fitted. Yes, I said, that's true although it's our business not yours. Well, he said, by my calculations that means you've got five floors in that house now and that's far too many for two cats: I shall move in too. Now. Now you hang on right there, I responded, access to the loft space does not an extra floor make, we've still got only four. Four! He said, quite scornfully, Larry. Four floors and look at the size of you Ghost, I bet you're not 4kg wet through, you could get hundreds of you in there. I've heard there's a very nice radiator on the top floor with room underneath for rolling about and exposing the fluffy underbelly.

Well, Larry, I'm afraid my hitherto faultless diplomatic façade cracked somewhat. You keep your underbelly away from my radiator, Mister, I said. You are *quite wrong*. That is not a big house. It is just very, very inconveniently shaped, which is why no-one wanted it and it was on the market for four years and the estate agent had given up. The only people daft enough to buy it were our Employees, and if Second Employee had not made questionable choices in life which culminated in her having to run away from Cambridge and her equity with nothing but a few pairs of knickers, some Tarot cards and a fake-fur coat in the back of a Punto then they would have bought a sensibly-shaped house in Bakewell or somewhere on the Hope

Valley Railway Line with one train an hour to Sheffield like normal people. So you can take your fluffy underbelly and sling your hook, because that is *my* radiator and *you* are *not having it*. And then I deployed the Tail. That showed him!

I strode back into our porch and I let out a cry of fury – MMMMRRRORROOOWWW!which immediately brought Esso and Second Employee running. This is where the potential breach of etiquette occurred, Larry. Second Employee took one look at me and said, my God, Ghost, are you alright, look at your tail. It is fluffed up like Basil Brush. I have never seen anything like it. And she took hold of my tail, and smoothed it right down. And it stayed smooth! I was so shocked, I looked up at Second Employee and smiled, which probably gave her the impression that what she had just done was Acceptable and not, in fact, Shocking. So this is what I would like to know, Larry: has Second Employee received specific training in Disarming the Diplomatic Service, or was she acting entirely independently? If the latter, I do not on balance think she acted with malice, so I would not like to have to take punitive measures: but nonetheless, we cannot have Employees Neutralising the Tail willy-nilly. Could you look up the appropriate Employee Development Strategic Framework and let me know? Many thanks, Larry, and I shall report back on any further developments!

April 2022

Larry and the Catinet. This is Esso, Ambassador to the High Peak, with my update. Well, Larry, things have been very eventful. Ghost and I performed an Extensive Stakeout this morning, to stop Interlopers coming in through the Catflap. Ghost says I was asleep, but I most definitely was not. I was resting my eyes and listening for intruders. Black and White Cat has been absolutely determined to move in recently. I discovered from talking to Grey Next Door Cat that the Jackdaws have been stirring up trouble, telling everyone about Ghost LOUNGING under her radiator 'as if she owns the place', and telling Black and White Cat there's definitely enough room under it for him as well. Well, as you can imagine, this is *most* unhelpful, and I have had to take a degree of punitive action. There was an incident: I now have a tiny wound on my ear, but I think it is fair to say that Black and White Cat has got the message. I shall approach the Jackdaws next, Larry, and let then know how unhelpful their interventions in this whole situation have been. It will be difficult to think of appropriate sanctions for the Jackdaws: they are terribly anarchic creatures, who seem to rely on nobody.

As you can imagine, after all that I have been very tired. Second Employee discovered me on the Guest Room bed and 'thought for a moment we'd acquired a round black cushion'. Well, of course it was not a cushion. it was me, and I reassured Second

Employee that she was in fact dealing with her old friend by purring loudly and narrowing my eyes. Besides. We've got more than enough cushions! In particular we've got some ridiculous ones with Embroidered Wasps which Second Employee got from the Factory Shop Rummage Sale when she was supposed to be looking for Running Leggings!

Also, Larry, I have had to have very strict words with Second Employee. She and First Employee are going to Spain next week to 'see how the house is doing' and Second Employee doesn't want to go, because she is not a brave or an adventurous Employee, and what she likes to do is mooch about at home, chatting to Ghost and I, and drinking coffee. Now, I have said to her that when one of the questionable choices you have made in life is marrying someone who was living a life of Shallow Ex-Pat Hedonism with Gin and Nudity in Andalucia just like on El Dorado, and then forcing him to live in the High Peak because you 'cannot bear to live anywhere where you can't wear a cardigan all year round', you have to go back to Andalucia occasionally to Deal With Things, and it is of no use sulking. Even though every time she goes to the house something goes wrong and she 'needed counselling after the incident involving the soil pipe'. Ghost and I really have heard quite enough about the incident involving the soil pipe. The soil pipe has now been replaced, and Second Employee cannot HARP on it forever. I have reassured her that Ghost and I will provide a high level of supervision to Interim Summer Employee for the very short length of time she is away, and that there is no need for anyone to mope about worrying about their seedlings and whether Ghost will miss her: even though Ghost is completely failing to follow the party line and has followed Second Employee round everywhere for the last forty-eight hours, making her eyes especially large and poignant.

It is possible, Larry, that Second Employee is about to break emotionally: Ghost says she really feels that she, personally, will be unable, ultimately, to resist the 'looking tragic in the suitcase manoeuvre', of which she is an acknowledged Virtuoso Performer; even though I have *specifically* requested she not do it this time because it is basically going to take a crowbar to get Second Employee to Manchester Airport to start with. Hopefully, Larry, we will be able to get the Employees off to do their Spanish Duty, keep Black and White Cat out of the Embassy, and think of an appropriate way to really bring home to the Jackdaws just how much trouble they have caused. The Ambassadorial Calling is not an easy one: but all I can do is try my best!

April 2022

Larry and the Catinet. This is Esso, Ambassador to the High Peak, with my update. Larry, I am very, very proud to report that every one of us, except Ghost, has Done Our Duty in the week just gone. The Employees have been to Spain to check on First

Employee's house, and Second Employee has been very brave and managed to stay there for a whole week without being silly about the terrifying roads and forcing First Employee to get flights back earlier, even though there is never enough 4G for him to deal with the Easyjet App, as the house is right at the top of a mountain. Larry, Second Employee says that despite the house being on a mountain, carved into a rock, 300 years old, and clearly haunted, she has decided to 'make is as comfortable and unchallenging as a Suburban Premier Inn, and as God is my witness I shall do it if it kills me, which it probably will, because it nearly has done so far'. Ghost says she does not know why Second Employee has this compulsion to take interesting, dramatic things and make them boring, but she has no doubt she will succeed, because look at First Employee, who lived a life of Perilous Excess and who now enjoys nothing more than a coffee and a fruit flapjack in the Wild Kettle Cafe at Hope Valley Garden Centre. So we have faith in Second Employee's ability to continue to generate Boredom, even internationally.

I have done my duty by keeping Black and White Cat at bay, and by chatting to Interim Summer Employee to keep him amused and occupied, and at no point did he ever become bitten very deeply by my teeth which is merely a scurrilous rumour. Indeed, I see myself as something as a Mentor to Interim Summer Employee, and I take a keen interest in the development of his Diplomatic Service Employee Skills. Interim

Summer Employee has also done his duty by Replenishing Biscuits When Appropriate, and watering all Second Employee's hundreds of plants, even the ones she had hidden in rooms no-one goes in very often.

I am afraid Ghost, however, was slightly difficult. Second Employee had told us they would be back on Tuesday, and as Tuesday wore on and on, Ghost began to feel anxious. Eventually she said to me, Esso, the Employees aren't coming back, they have tricked me, and I shall never knead on Second Employee's middle again while she reassures me that I am still the softest cat in the entirety of the High Peak. Perhaps she has found an even softer cat in Spain, who is kneading on her middle right at this moment. I am going out to tell Black and White Cat he can have my radiator, because what use is a radiator to me now when everything is Dust and Ashes. So she went out through the Catflap, strode right up to Black and White Cat and opened her mouth, but luckily right at that moment Second Employee appeared and called to us through the back door. So instead of giving away her radiator, Ghost shouted to Black and White Cat 'hey you over there with your stupid hairy tail' and ran back inside to say hello to the Employees. Now, Larry, I find myself with a degree of diplomatic awkwardness. I have tried to finesse the situation by apologising to Black and White Cat, but, secretly, I must confess that I wish Ghost had taken the opportunity of her (unmerited, as we now know) emotional *crise de nerfs* to shout something useful, like 'hey you over there bugger off and stop trying to move in', rather than resorting to cheap personal insults. No matter. We struggle on, Larry, with our territory negotiations and our continued attempts to improve the Employees: I don't wish to complain, but surely *soon* it will get easier!

April 2022

Larry and the Catinet: this is Ghost, Ambassador to the High Peak, with my update. Larry, I understand Esso has written an UTTERLY DISINGENUOUS report suggesting I was the only one who did not do my duty while the Employees were away being ridiculous in Spain and frankly probably for most of the time mooching about drinking coffee in coffee places which they could have done in England anyway, without leaving me all on my own, with no-one to stroke or love me at all. So I have had WORDS with Esso. This is what actually happened: Second Employee told me before she left, and she had promised, and kissed my fur and crossed her heart and everything: that she would be back on Tuesday and I was not to worry. Well, what time did she eventually rock up at the back door, calling me? Five minutes to midnight. So although that is *technically* within the bounds of her promise, I really feel it is not in the spirit of the whole thing; and who knew that Second Employee was capable of being awake after 11:30pm in any case, because the last time she was up after that time she ordered a book about cakes on Amazon even though she keeps telling people she has given up sugar, and then didn't remember doing it in the morning. Or: *so she says*. So any cat in my position would have felt unsettled, and Esso is actually lucky I didn't say anything worse to Black and White Cat. Very lucky.

Especially given that, the night before, Esso and Black and White Cat had had a Big Fight! And Esso got a cut on his ear! And Interim Summer Employee messaged Second Employee with a photo of it! And Larry, that is not all. A few days before that, Interim Summer Employee became very, very deeply bitten by Esso's teeth and bled quite a lot, and messaged Second Employee to say that he thought Esso had 'opened a vein' but that 'it was fine because it wasn't fatal'. Larry, Esso says if Employees become bitten by his teeth occasionally, that is one of those things which must just be dealt with and we will merely add it to the Employee Training Plan: but I think, frankly, that Esso's teeth do not bite people on their own, because Esso is attached to them, and he must take some level of responsibility.

And this next thing is the worst of all, Larry. Obviously, First Employee had heard all the dramatic story from Interim Summer Employee, and he stroked Esso and said, well Mr Esso Puss Puss Cat (which is Esso's formal name for formal occasions), I don't think this sounds like behaviour fit for an

Ambassador, going scruffing round the neighbourhood, fighting people. The indignity of an Employee saying such a thing! So, Larry, I think *technically* Esso has brought the dignified Ambassadorial Office into disrepute, and *technically* he could be sacked and I could have all his biscuits. But I do not wish to invoke the formal disciplinary procedure at this stage because if someone needs to fight Black and White Cat again I would rather it was not me. So I will wait to see if Esso annoys me in the future and then it might be useful to have something on him. Thank you, Larry! (p.s. Second Employee is being very silly and has refused to believe anything bad of Esso in any way. She says since she has come back, Esso has spent the entire time on the sofa next to her with all his legs in the air, purring, and he is a 'lovely gentle cat and not the neighbourhood scrapper as certain people have misrepresented him'. Larry, I don't know why Second Employee does not realise that her skills in Making Dramatic Things Boring also extend to Esso: and that Esso is not the same when he is outside facing down the worst of the North Buxton Bad Cat Posse. But until I have taught her to understand a little more Cat, she will have to remain innocent!)

April 2022

Larry, a quick update from me, Esso, Ambassador to the High Peak, to share a point of best practice. Members of the Catinet: it's very important that we always remember our Employees are weak, silly creatures, whose brains are very tiny, and make allowances accordingly; otherwise things can go wrong. For example, when Second Employee becomes overwhelmed with the cutthroat, fast-paced world of Embassy Employment she 'has a strop', as Ghost calls it, and says, I shall go and stay in a Travelodge and then where will you all be. Then she looks on the Internet at how much Travelodges cost these days, even ones which are in the High Peak and not in Central London, and decides she would rather spend the money on something quite different; for example more Denby Arabesque, or Aerial Yoga sessions in Chesterfield, both of which contribute *absolutely nothing* to her effectiveness in her role. And obviously while we are going through this process it is not conducive to Employee or Ambassador Morale. So, one of the things I do is to make sure I am there to support Second Employee emotionally through difficult situations. For instance, today I watched her very carefully from the dresser while she made some digestive biscuits. This is because the window cleaner was here, who makes a very, very alarming sound with his squirty pole thing, and who goes crashing about in quite a terrifying manner. I was concerned that Second Employee might not be able to weather the emotional storm on her own, and so I kept a supportive eye on her, with the result that she managed to produce her biscuits, even though her dough was a bit soggy, and kept her mind off things. This is just one example of my dedication to Development of Employees, even Employees with tiny brains and a sad lack of intellectual interests. I hope the other members of the Catinet find this advice useful.

I'm afraid when I discussed it with Ghost she was most unhelpful. She said, it is you who is frightened of the window cleaner, Esso, I didn't even notice he was here because I was upstairs under my radiator thinking great thoughts: for example what will be the long-term political implications of Elon Musk taking over Twitter: and also is it true what Grey Next Door Cat is saying about Bauhaus being the next trend in Interiors, because if it is I *dread to think* what Second Employee will do with colour blocking on our first-floor landing. And also Second Employee is only making digestive biscuits because she is pretending to be on a diet again, but give her till Saturday and she'll be right there making something appalling with buttercream and Biscoff spread.

Well, Larry, what Ghost said is quite untrue, except possibly about Second Employee and the digestives: what actually made my eyes wide today was not fear, but glancing at a Private Eye on top of the recycling pile while I was on the dresser. I was shocked that such cynicism exists. I have therefore decided to ban Second Employee from reading political satire, because I think at this stage it is unhelpful, and can only lead to Discontent. I am going to suggest to her instead that she takes out a subscription to the People's Friend: it has a wholesome mix of knitting patterns, recipes, and instructive stories about Female Employees falling in love with the new vet and his adorable labrador. It may even be that it contains a crossword she is able to do, because when she was last at the house in Spain, she discovered that the crossword she had been unable to complete in Take A Break and had left from last time had been completed by friends who had stayed there a few weeks ago: and now she 'feels inadequate'. Employees are so sensitive and irrational, Larry, but until we can open the tins ourselves we unfortunately have no choice but to attempt to all get along!

May 2022

Larry, and the Catinet, this is a very disturbed Ghost, Ambassador to the High Peak. Larry, I am INCREDULOUS. Esso has FORCED Second Employee to buy the People's Friend because he says it is wholesome and suitable, but I have perused it carefully and this month there is a RIDICULOUS story about an Employee who wants to paint her sitting room purple and whose partner, after being sensible and leaving her over it, suddenly decides that she is a wonderful person who brings colour to his life and they can have the sitting room purple as long as they have beige curtains. Larry, this is the absolute worst thing that Second Employee could possibly read. I have told Esso he can keep his suggestions for reading matter to himself in future, and unless he can absolutely guarantee that the next edition of The People's Friend is going to feature stories about Employees who suddenly realise that their cats leaving out the Farrow and Ball paint chart with Ammonite displayed prominently is *not coincidental*, I shall suggest reading matter to her myself, and we will begin with How To Be A Better Employee magazine. Esso says this magazine does not actually exist, but clearly that is a minor point, so Larry, could you make sure it exists and is widely distributed in supermarkets before Second Employee goes to Waitrose next Sunday. Many thanks.

Also, and Larry, this is particularly annoying: after Esso did his sharing of Best Practice, I also wanted to tell people about my own, which is much better than Esso's. I refer to my patented move, the Passive-Aggressive Slinky. I shall explain. When Second Employee puts flea medication on my neck, it annoys me, and for a couple of days afterwards when I approach her and she puts a hand out to stroke me I SLINK my furry back away from her in a fluid movement and then look at her pointedly, as if to say, how DARE you approach, you flea-medication-wielding monster. Thus, Second Employee delays our flea medication, because she cannot face the Passive-Aggressive Slinky, and we have to deal with the whole situation less often. I really am clever. Everyone says so, especially Soft Grey Next Door Cat who is trying to learn it himself although I personally don't think he has the flexibility in his thoracic spine. Anyway, I told Esso I was going to explain this to the Catinet in the spirit of skill-sharing, and he said, actually he had been worrying about it! Because, apparently, sometimes he sits with the Employees when they are talking, and before Second Employee became our Rescue Employee she used to live with a man who also took offence at things she did: for example, when she spoke at times outside the permitted slot which was 8:55pm-9pm, or failed to cook dinner quickly enough when she had flu, or once when she ate two biscuits: but instead of doing the Passive-Aggressive Slinky, which is skilled and completely justified, he did things like not talking to her for weeks at a time, or punching walls, or shouting things at her that Esso would not tell me what they were. And Esso says he is not entirely sure, even though she has now been our Rescue Employee for a long time, whether Second Employee is quite psychologically robust enough for the Passive-Aggressive Slinky. And I should stop doing it.

So, Larry, I am discombobulated, as you can imagine. Luckily, I think Second Employee's grasp of Cat is now good enough, so I shall say to her that she now lives somewhere lovely, with magnificent Ambassadors and with First Employee who all love her despite her execrable taste in interior decoration and inexplicable fondness for dungarees, and so she has got to do her duty and stop *brooding* about the past. And also I shall ask her how she has managed to go from living somewhere where she was not allowed to speak at all apart from five minutes a day to marrying First Employee, who has chatted non-stop since 'the minute the ink was dry on the marriage certificate' and who even talks in his sleep. Esso and I wonder if she might have been better starting off with someone good-natured but quiet, as a way of reacclimatising to the human race.

And my message to all Employees is, if they are also in a situation where this kind of thing happens to them, they should try not to be in it for much longer: because they may, in the future, acquire a very fine Ambassador, such as me: and that Ambassador may, quite legitimately, fairly, and appropriately, need to manipulate them by piling huge amounts of guilt on them: and the Ambassador should be able to do that with a clear conscience and an acknowledgment of their skill! Larry, the situations these Employees get themselves into! Still, it makes Esso and I happy to think that we have taken on Rescue Employees and given them a better life, even if we do consequently have to compromise on the efficiency of the delivery of the High Peak Embassy Stategic Plan!

May 2022

Larry, Esso here, Ambassador to the High Peak, with my report. Larry, we have had a challenging week. Many of us, mostly me, have faced great hardship. It is lucky that Ghost, I, and First Employee (obviously to a much lesser extent) continue to be models of Duty and Emotional Resilience, because Second Employee really isn't doing well at the moment. Apparently Second Employee still half-owns a house in Cambridge, which her ex-partner has refused to leave, but which she has now got to sell this year. Unfortunately her ex-partner is a hoarder who has not cleaned or repaired anything since the day Second Employee ran away five years ago, because he believes it to be Second Employee's Duty to have stayed and cleaned, although this is incorrect. Because it is *actually* Second Employee's Duty to be an Employee for Ghost and I, however dubious her skills might be on this front. Anyway, Second Employee asked an estate agent to visit to give her a valuation this week and it did not go well. She says she does not care about the money, but she cannot take the pity: and she is thinking of having postcards printed of our Embassy and handing them out to interested parties to prove that she herself lives in sanitary conditions, because the way things are going she can see she is practically going to have to hold group therapy sessions of traumatised estate agents after each valuation.

Well, Larry, Ghost says this is sarcasm and Second Employee is not really going to have postcards printed, but if she does, I will make sure they feature Ghost and I very prominently because we are obviously the best, most hygienic, and most stylish items in the Embassy Interior. Ghost is very rude and has said to me that it would be best to keep me out of the putative postcards as 'you get black hair over everything, Esso, and you're the reason we have to have all those silly throws on the sofa downstairs after the Employees took absolute leave of their senses and brought a white sofa into the house with a black cat'. Well, this is quite untrue: my fur is fine and delicate and silky and doesn't stick to anything, and is not at all like 'thick black velcro floating about everywhere' as Ghost says.

Ghost has had difficulties this week, too, because a very large Wood Pigeon has taken to strutting about our garden NIBBLING on the plants: and Ghost feels duty bound to attempt to disrupt this process. We thought we would never miss the quick cunning of the Naughty Jackdaws: but Ghost says explaining to Ms Woodpigeon why she must not nibble the Rosemary until it establishes is 'like talking to a brick wall', and she is becoming increasingly frustrated.

I am the main one, though, Larry, who has faced hardship this week! Second Employee was sitting on the sofa the other night crying because her house has been destroyed, and First Employee was sitting next to her, saying, come on Susie, we have to be cheerful and optimistic, just like we were when we moved into this house and found a dead rat underneath the oven, do you remember. We were cheerful and robust about it and now the kitchen is spotless and the dead rat is just a funny anecdote. Well, Larry, I was quite furious: because if I had been sitting next to First Employee, not only would she not have had to listen about dead rats which will surely not cheer anyone up, but I would have been on my special soft blanket which is my favourite and which Second Employee bought especially for me from Morrisons. But First Employee was in my way! He said, come and sit next to me, Esso, look, there's room: but Second Employee rightly observed that I take after her side of the family, none of whom are able to sit next to each other on sofas, which causes all sorts of issues when they visit each other. So I had to sit on the piano stool and wait until the Employees wandered into the garden to be confused about why the Rosemary is not establishing as quickly as it should be (although Ghost is trying her best!) and I could reclaim my blanket. Ghost says I was sulking, but I was not. I was merely waiting. Sometimes, Larry, it is best to wait, strategically; perhaps on a piano stool, in a sunbeam, with our eyes closed. We shall continue to keep the twin suns of Diplomacy and Culture shining in the High Peak, and hope for a better week to come!

May 2022

Larry and the Catinet, Esso here, Ambassador to the High Peak. Larry, after my previous update, Ghost has told me off. I do think it is a little unjustified but I'm updating again just to correct any misunderstandings. She was very firm with me. She said, for God's sake Esso, here we all are in complete crisis with Second Employee flopping around sobbing about her Cambridge house not having been hoovered and barely carrying out her duties, First Employee depressing us all by reminding us about the dead rat in the kitchen, and me devoting HOURS trying to stop that infernal wood pigeon nibbling that damned rosemary plant, and all you can think about is your bloody blanket and not being able to sit on it for twenty minutes. Esso you are like the Mr Pooter of the Feline Diplomatic Service and you need to pull your head out of your fundament and look at what is going on around you. Well, Larry, I don't think I need to tell you how shocked I am at Ghost's language! I have most certainly had words with her. But, just in case you read this and think, well, Ghost has got a point, I would just like to emphasise to you that my blanket really is very, very soft, and that it was bought for me specially by Second Employee from Morrisons, and so any cat - any cat - would be unhappy about being prevented from sitting on it, for however short a period. So my suffering was very real.

Anyway, I am pleased to report that Second Employee has rallied. I have told her that members of the Catinet were supportive of her troubles, and she has found this cheering. Also, luckily for her, although possibly not for us, she has realised something with far-reaching implications; N.B. that although she has now painted everything which could reasonably be painted inside the house, there are quite a few things outside which have so far escaped her attentions. So she is distracting herself by painting the new shed before it is erected. She has chosen a rather subtle shade of duck-egg blue, and Ghost and I both hoped this might herald a new era of Good Taste, but she then suggested it might look nice with 'bright pink accents', which it most certainly will not. But in the circumstances we are trying to be supportive. She is also knitting mittens with a complicated skull design on them. Ghost says this is not a good sign, psychologically, but I say, if she is sublimating a desire to kill people by knitting skulls then that is a perfectly reasonable thing to do and much less trouble for us than the alternative. Obviously it is not great to have Employees generating Woolly Memento Moris all over the place, but perhaps she can dispose of the mittens by giving them to Interim Summer Employee or someone with similarly large hands, because Second Employee, ironically, despite being a Rather Tense Employee, especially at the moment, is often unable to get a tight tension in her knitting and apparently they 'do not make needles any smaller'. So that is that, Larry, and if the mittens end up like large deaths-head oven gloves we will just have to put the whole thing down to Second Employee's slightly disturbed psychological state at the moment. Never mind, Larry! I think we have weathered the crisis, and although it is true that Ghost's struggles with Ms Woodpigeon are ongoing, we are looking forward to a more constructive weekend!

May 2022

Larry and the Catinet. Ghost here, Ambassador to the High Peak, with my update. Well, Larry, I have barely had the energy or the time to provide this update. Since you last heard from me, sleep and I have been strangers. I am barely getting my twenty-two hours a day. There are BIRDIES nesting in the roof of the Embassy. Yes. BIRDIES. BIRDIES! I am monitoring the situation almost without cease from the top floor. I don't mean to make comparisons: but, during my Constant Vigil, certain cats {*cough* Esso *cough*} have been spending their time on blankets with their LEGGIES in the air. Esso says he has put himself temporarily in charge of Employee Morale, and is nuzzling up against Second Employee, who has had a migraine and spent all of Monday on the sofa next to him, to 'make her feel better'. I have told Esso there is other useful work he could be doing, but he says, 'Ghost, you need to examine your feelings about constructed gender roles and whether you might be behind the times, because as a large chunky male cat I too can be affectionate, and it is perfectly legitimate for me to spend the whole day kneading on and chirruping at Second Employee. She is only getting migraines because she is stressed.'

Stressed! When she's not monitored a single BIRDY! Larry, Second Employee is getting migraines because she keeps bringing HOARDS of people back to the Embassy and feeding them cake and coffee, and she knows she is not a robust enough Employee for that amount of sugar and caffeine. And also they all try to touch me and say, look, what a pretty cat but she doesn't want to talk to us. Well, no, I do *not* want to talk to random visitors! I'm busy! There are BIRDIES!

Obviously, Larry, I do not wish to draw, even by implication, any comparison between my and Esso's respective levels of commitment to the delivery of the High Peak Feline Diplomatic Plan 2022-2023. I only ask you to consider the facts contained in this update, and therefore which of us might be the one in line for a transfer to Derbyshire Dales in time for the winter. That is all. Also, Larry, in the time I have not been monitoring BIRDIES I have been supervising First Employee, who has been getting things out of the old shed, and putting things back into the new shed. I have made sure everything, especially First Employee, has been touched very carefully with my nose at each stage of the proceedings, as is proper. Of course, Larry, my efforts have not been appreciated. On entering the kitchen yesterday, I heard Second Employee say to First Employee 'has Ghostycat been helping you?' and First Employee reply 'she's been hindering me and she's nearly tripped me up a few times on the stairs and killed me, haven't you, Mrs Nosy Noser?'. Well, Larry, I would like it set down in the High Peak Diplomatic Records that if the Employees had organised the man who re-concreted the top patio bit and the stairs outside a bit better and not allowed the whole affair to become the Saga it did, we might not have steps which are all completely different sizes and a complete deathtrap for Lumbering Employees although not for stealthy Ambassadors: and also, I object formally to the nickname Mrs Nosy Noser which I notice being used of me occasionally, because it is utterly inaccurate, as I am in fact a cat who is known for my interest in purely cerebral things.

Thank you. Honestly, Larry, I don't like to boast, but if it hadn't been for my tireless efforts in the last week this Embassy would be in an even worse shape than it is. I shall be concentrating my efforts in the coming days on making sure Esso and Second Employee stop lazing about self-indulgently, pretending to be 'having migraine auras' and 'deconstructing gender expectations' and get some proper work done!

May 2022

Larry and the Catinet: Ghost here, Ambassador to the High Peak. Larry, Second Employee has indeed painted pink accents on the almost-tasteful shed! Honestly, I can't bear to look at it. Esso says, look Ghost, leave it for now, she's not at her best, it can always be painted over in due course. But honestly, Larry, I think Second Employee needs to know what creatures with a proper aesthetic sense think of her and her accent colours, so I made sure to make that point strongly to her via my Stern Expression. What makes me FURIOUS, Larry, is that I have myself with my own very pretty ears heard Second Employee tell visitors with a look of apology that she was in the middle of tidying a table 'and that is why it's a tip' - honestly, Larry, it makes the whole thing worse! She can worry about a pile of magazines, which is obviously just temporary, but go out and deface a shed, which is permanent, whatever Esso says! Unless Esso thinks he is going to go out and hold a paintbrush between his paws and sort it out! Which he isn't, because as he well knows, the last time we tried that we couldn't get the lid off the paint. Apparently you need a screwdriver.

Anyway, Esso and I have been considering the issue of Bodily Autonomy for Ambassadors, and we're going to have to ask you, Larry, to issue an Emergency Edict that Employees do not touch the FEETIES of Ambassadors, however tempting it is. Esso says he was lying on his blanket the other evening, next to Second Employee, with his legs in the air and his front legs stretched out over his head to grab Second Employee with his claws. He says he thinks the fur of his Underneath was probably rippling very invitingly, but this does not excuse what transpired. He heard Second Employee say to First Employee, as she was trying to detach Esso from her jumper, 'look at the cat on his back with all his legs in the air. Doesn't he look sweet. It makes me want to ruffle the fur on his middle'. Esso says he wasn't too concerned about this statement, because we both know that Second Employee has had a healthy respect for the Underneaths of Ambassadors ever since the incident in 2004 which involved Aunty Kath, Wine, Beowulf the Feisty Long-Haired Ginger, and consequent TCP. But then First Employee looked at him and said, 'yes, look at that Fabulous Cat. If he does that when he's next to me, I shall grab him by his Feeties and I shall wobble them up and down'.

Now, Larry: I'm sure you understand that Esso and I cannot continually monitor the position of our Feeties with respect to

First Employee, especially Esso, who is prone to being overtaken by unexpected naps: but I think we can all agree that having them grabbed and 'wobbled up and down' is a humiliation we should never, never have to endure. Could you make sure First Employee knows this is utterly unacceptable, please, by whatever means necessary. Perhaps you could inform Second Employee, as she is normally very good at telling him firmly which of his impulses are inappropriate, and recently had a success at the Waitrose Checkout where he was moaning loudly about the woman in front FAFFING, and she had to say, Darling, everyone can hear you with your loud voice, and when this woman turns round and punches you I am not going to rescue you. So be quiet. And he was. Although Second Employee says, the woman he was complaining about would not have turned round and punched him because actually he was right, she was a terrible FAFFER, and it would have taken her 20 minutes to decide which fist to use, by which time both the Employees would have been back and unpacking all the massive amounts of kale they buy every week which Second Employee does not then want to eat. So technically he was right, but he is not even technically right about our Feeties, Larry, so please can you ensure the Edict is communicated quickly! Many thanks, and we will try to bear the awful pink shed until Esso works out how to get some proper leverage on that screwdriver!

May 2022

Larry and the Catinet. This is Ghost, Ambassador to the High Peak. Larry, this is not a proper, intellectual, useful update of the kind you've come to expect from me. Second Employee has asked if I will notify the Catinet that she has finished knitting her very silly Skull Mittens, which are now complete, and which she is going to give to some poor family member for Christmas as soon as she identifies someone with big enough hands. I have told her that this is an Ambassadorial Update: it is not Show and Tell: and that if exceptions are made I do not know where it will end. Esso has a great deal more patience than me with this sort of nonsense, but, unfortunately for Second Employee, he is out for his after-dinner patrol of the perimeter, and briefly unavailable. Anyway, I instructed her to lay the ridiculous mittens on the piano stool so I could see them better and assess whether or not I considered them worth showing: I concluded I did not, mainly because I really do not think her Latvian Braid is very competently executed. No matter. Second Employee would like the Catinet's Employees to know that knitting mittens is a 'nice, calming thing to do', and that if anyone else would like to sublimate their stress by knitting skulls rather than drinking Gin, eating cake, or driving too fast down the A6 to Chesterfield, for example, the pattern is free and is available on the internet. I think it would be better, Catinet, for you to instruct your Employees not to waste time on knitting mittens, painting sheds pink, attempting to grow a courgette, creating home-made Jaffa Cakes, or any of the other utterly ridiculous things Second Employee spends her time doing. The proper function of an Employee is to follow their Departmental Strategic Plan, stroke members of the Catinet on demand, and to open the Dreamies packet!

May 2022

Larry, this is Esso, Ambassador to the High Peak, with my update. Larry, I'm sorry I've allowed Ghost to do the last few updates. I hope you don't feel I've been neglecting my Duty: I've been extremely busy, patrolling our perimeters and keeping First Employee away from my Feeties: but I do sometimes feel Ghost allows a note of Cynicism to creep into her reports, which is not the image we should project. But no matter! I'm back now with my cheery (yet always professional) optimism. I spent last night LOUNGING on my back with Second Employee, happy and relaxed, because I trust her implicitly not to grab my FEETIES: but, even so, there had been a very small contretemps earlier. I had successfully persuaded an adolescent Jackdaw to accompany me into the Embassy to begin diplomatic talks. Obviously there had been an outside risk that he might become very slightly bitten, or indeed crunched right up, by my teeth; but in the interests of Feline-Corvid relations we decided jointly it was a risk we were both willing to take. However, surprisingly and disappointingly, some of his older relatives disagreed, which led to quite a Kerfuffle and to Second Employee characterising what happened next as 'my God, the cat has just escaped a horde of Squawking Jackdaws and run through the catflap with a little one in his mouth like something off Chariots of Fire'. Very unfortunately, because of Second Employee Faffing and Flapping About, me and the youngster became separated somewhere near the Dining Room Sofa. First Employee wrapped him up in a teatowel and restored him to his agitated compatriots, who were briefly mollified: but I think we should ask ourselves the following, Larry; without us being willing to take risks, how can diplomatic progress ever be made? No matter, I am regrouping today while it is raining and will resume my diplomatic efforts with the Jackdaws tomorrow!

Also, Larry, I don't know if you have heard anything about this, but Second Employee is muttering about a 'cost of living crisis', and told Ghost that when she went to Waitrose yesterday for 'rinse aid and watercress and the other bits she can't get in Aldi' lots of things had actually gone up 10p even from the week before. First Employee says it is like 'shopping in the Weimar Republic'. We are not sure where the Weimar Republic is, Larry, have you heard of it? Ghost is going to nip out later and ask Grey Next Door Cat if he knows, because he has lots of local knowledge. Ghost says it is probably somewhere on the other side of Glossop, but I think it is almost certainly next door to Cheadle Hulme. Anyway, Larry, Second Employee says she is 'entirely 50-50 between starting civil unrest or starting a commune'. Well, I would like to reassure you, Larry, that we shall Clamp Down Immediately on any signs of civil unrest among Embassy employees, although Ghost says there is absolutely no chance of Second Employee even starting a mild protest because she would insist on breaking everything off after half an hour for tea and biscuits. Obviously this is reassuring, although I really don't like the idea of Second Employee having leanings towards Self-Sufficient Communes either, because I strongly suspect that her idea of such a thing would involve tie-dyeing and possibly a Ukulele, and that there would be no-one among her relatives or friends who would be capable of wringing the neck of a chicken. Anyway, Larry, clearly the Cost Of Living Crisis is nonsense, because our food is still plentiful and my blanket is still in situ. Although Ghost did hear First Employee saying the other day 'if we have to turn the heating off next winter and strap a cat to our fronts instead, I'm bagsying Esso because he's chunkier and more biddable'. Ghost says she can't decide whether she should be offended by this or not, and frankly, Larry, nor can I – so we're going to both have a nice rest and take a few days to consider things!

Chapter 6

Summer 2022: Sausage Rolls and Demonic Cakes

June 2022

Larry and the Catinet. This is Ghost here, and I am not *actually* 'rushing to do this update just to say I told you so', like Esso says I am. That is not my motivation at all! I merely thought we could all learn from the events of this Jubilee Weekend. Especially Esso. Because I have been telling him where he has been going wrong for *ages*!

Anyway, it began badly, when Second Employee invited some of her family to a Jubilee Celebration Lunch, and then couldn't remember if they were actually Republicans, or if everyone had run out of energy for that kind of thing somewhere among all the difficulties of Covid, Energy Bills, and Oat Milk going up to £2 in Waitrose. So she changed it to a Simultaneous Jubilee Celebration and Ironically Subversive Jubilee Non-Celebration Lunch, which, as you know, Larry, is a very difficult event to cater for, as the etiquette is unclear. So Second Employee's Mother said she would make a Celebration/ Non-Celebration Cake, and Second Employee was not to worry. But instead of not worrying, Second Employee for some reason became OBSESSED with making sausage rolls, and spent the

ENTIRETY of Thursday making Rough Puff Pastry; which as you know, Larry, no-one bothers with these days because it is a massive FAFF and you can buy Actual Puff Pastry in the Supermarket, in a convenient block. I do not know why Second Employee gets these ideas into her head. Anyway, she grated her frozen butter and said rude words about the grater, Buxton, First Employee, and the Cost of Living Increase which meant she couldn't just 'buy a lot of nibbles from Marks and Spencer and crack on like a normal person', and then Second Employee's Mother rang and said she had burnt her cake and 'literally didn't care because she was having an enormous glass of wine and eating crisps'. Then Second Employee said some more things which were not helpful or at all in line with her Workplan, and said she was giving up and going to bed.

Well, it was good that the Employees got a good night's sleep, because in the morning Second Employee's mother WhatsApped Second Employee an hour before everyone was due to arrive and told her she had invited quite a few more family members, and they were all coming too, which was nice. So the Employees rushed about trying to create a Running Buffet out of whatever was left in the fridge. At least we had lots of sausage rolls!

Anyway, Larry, this brings me to the Crucial Point of my Update. Every one of Second Employee's Family came in, looked at Esso, and said in hushed tones, is that the cat who

Bit Paul, who is Second Employee's Father. Every Single One. And Second Employee's brother stroked me and said yes, and it definitely wasn't Ghost, because look how lovely and gentle she is. And that was very accurate, Larry, because I am lovely and gentle and the softest cat in the whole of the High Peak as proved through objective collection of data. And so when Esso says that it is no problem when sometimes his teeth bite people, because barely anyone notices and certainly no-one remembers; that is not *entirely* true, because clearly Esso has attained the status of Dark Legend among Second Employee's family. Which is hardly a triumph for our Joint Diplomacy! Esso and I discussed whether, as an emergency measure, it would be diplomatically expedient for me to trip up Second Employee's Father on the Terrible Garden Steps, not seriously but just perhaps to make him stumble slightly and take the attention off Esso: but we decided this was just too dangerous. Besides, Second Employee says her father must be kept alive and healthy at all costs, because he has a Toby Jug in the shape of Mr Micawber which he has promised to leave her in his will, and she is determined to not inherit it for as long as possible.

I hope you have found my update helpful, Larry. It goes without saying that I tell you this about Esso's teeth more in sorrow than in anger. I will discuss the issue further with Esso when he is not being so ridiculously defensive! Also, can you believe Second Employee doesn't actually like sausage rolls? Hopefully the whole affair was just a temporary madness and we can get on tomorrow with the proper delivery of the High Peak Strategic Plan!

June 2022

Larry and the Catinet. Esso, Joint Ambassador to the High Peak, here, with a very important update. As an aside, Larry, Second Employee has mentioned to me that she is having difficulty taking photographs of me for the Embassy Files which are commensurate with the Importance and Seriousness of my Role and Person. I acknowledge this may be an issue. Second Employee and I are, of course, BFFs, so when she approaches me with her phone I automatically roll onto my back so she can stroke my furry tummy. I believe it is called a Pavlovian response. I may suggest to Second Employee that she let First Employee take the photographs instead, as earlier today he touched one of my Feeties (I was on my back on my blanket, extended one leg elegantly in the air, and he grabbed it! Like a Sneaky Opportunist!) so with him I am more guarded. And also he has got a better camera on his phone, whereas Second Employee has got a crappy old thing which barely functions because she keeps dropping it and the memory is full of photos of Ghost and I, and whenever First Employee says why don't we get you a better phone she says, I can't be bothered to get used to another one but are we spending money, because if we are I might buy a spinning wheel. As ever, Second Employee has entirely the wrong attitude.

Anyway, I have something very disturbing to report to you, Larry. It has been First Employee's birthday this week, and Second Employee made him a cake. Ghost and I understand that Employees have a very silly custom whereby, when they have made a Birthday Cake, they insert into the top of it small brightly-coloured candles, and set light to them while singing a quite repetitive song rather tunelessly. This was covered in the Training Course which Ghost and I attended as kittens, *Understanding Ridiculous & Pointless Employee Customs*, which we have often consulted our notes from and which has proved very useful. However, Second Employee appears to have gone a little further this year. I was sitting (on my blanket) when she produced a Terrifying Sparkly Thing, which First Employee lit because Second Employee is nervous of matches after her childhood which was spent with her cousins who used to set fire to dustbins. It went FFFFFFZZZZZZZ SPARK SPARK SPARK WHHHIIIZZZZ, oh Larry I cannot convey the terror in words, and, as the Employees observed, my eyes 'went enormous'.

Well, yes, Larry, I was extremely alarmed! It was clear to me that the Terrifying Sparkly Thing, far from being just 'a dodgy cake sparkler which Second Employee got on eBay', was Terrifying Enough to risk Summoning the Devil: and honestly,

Second Employee unknowingly working with Dark Energies is *all we need* at this juncture. Luckily, this time, I am fairly sure that the Dark Energies remained Unwoken: but Larry, I would like to request that Second Employee be allowed, as a special dispensation, to join the other very useful training course Ghost and I attended as kittens, *How to Summon the Devil Then Send Him Back When You're Fed Up Of Him*, because if she *is* going to rampage about willy-nilly doing this kind of thing, we would rather she does it within a framework of Proper Knowledge. I know this may be a controversial request, Larry, in that we do not normally open up Everyday Feline Knowledge to Employees: but Ghost and I are both willing to to vouch for Second Employee, or, at least to assure you that her intentions are usually good although they sometimes (often) exceed her abilities.

I would like to request, though, that she do the course over Zoom rather than going to London: because we can't really spare her overnight from her duties, and also if she goes to London there is the danger of her wandering off to Liberty and buying fabric, which she most definitely can't afford. Many thanks, Larry! If you could get one of your Employees to send the Zoom link to me that would be fantastic: esso@highpeakembassy.gov.uk. I just can't trust Second Employee to check her email regularly!

June 2022

Larry and the Catinet, this is Ghost, Ambassador to the High Peak, with my update which is always more useful than Esso's I think we have to acknowledge. Well, Larry, I have two things to tell you about, one of which is sensible because it is about me, and one of which is RIDICULOUS because it involves Second Employee. Firstly, I have taken over Esso's blanket. This is to teach him emotional resilience in line with the High Peak Embassy Ambassador and Staff Moral Development Strategy, 22-23. I have started with Esso because honestly, I look at the Employees, and there is so much work to do on their Moral Development that we are going to need to extend the strategy into 23-34 and possibly 24-25. Even with Esso I haven't been completely successful yet, because what I'm finding is that he sneaks straight back on it when I pop outside to make sure Second Employee is putting Tomorite on her tomatoes (she isn't, she's got some silly organic concoction from B&Q which isn't as good!). But Larry, you can be completely reassured that I am intending to persevere in this.

The second RIDICULOUS thing is that Second Employee's entire family *without exception* has gone mad with regards to sausage rolls. Esso and I are frankly a little worried. First, Second Employee became OBSESSED with making sausage rolls over the Jubilee Weekend, to the exclusion of all other useful things, which she then refused to eat because she doesn't actually like sausage rolls, she just 'felt they were appropriate'. Then, when Esso was doing his weekly perusal of Social Media Accounts Connected to Second Employee's Friends and Associates (Second Employee is extremely prone to social contagion, so we keep an eye on her influences in order to head off silly ideas if necessary), he discovered that her brother, who is a hyper-realist painter, has painted one, albeit from a shop! Larry, how has Second Employee managed to have a brother who is a hyper-realist painter to start with? Honestly, it's typical of her. I personally think she has done it on purpose. It's not a proper occupation. I disapprove of this very strongly. Could you pass a law or something to make Second Employee's brother have a proper job, something perhaps involving an excel spreadsheet, or a Toolbox: or, if he is going to persist in his Silliness, could you make him paint Proper Things? Perhaps fields with sheep in them, flowers, or white cats with extremely pretty markings, and very specifically not sausage rolls, which are not an appropriate subject for Art. Are there sausage rolls on the ceiling of the Sistine Chapel, Larry? There are not. Does the Pompidou hold an annual Interpretations of the Sausage Roll in Art Retrospective? It does not. Is there a room in the Louvre called La Salle Des Beaux Rouleaux de Saucisse? There is not. Does MoMA in New York hold a collection of the finest contemporary Sausage Roll Paintings with an emphasis on Cubism? Actually, I'm not entirely sure it doesn't, so don't quote me on that one, but: my point stands. *What is it* with Second Employee's Family and sausage rolls? So, if Second Employee's mother or someone is at this very moment working on a design for making earrings out of sausage rolls or using them as a fuel substitute in an eco-car or something even worse, can you make sure that doesn't happen. Thank you.

Thank you, Larry, I don't know why I try to keep up standards of Gracious Living when I am undermined and resisted at every turn but I am just not a cat who can turn a blind eye to Inadequacies. I shall continue, although it feels like an uphill struggle, and I shall update again soon!

Larry, this is Esso... Larry, could you possibly ask Ghost to stop teaching me emotional resilience, please?

June 2022

Larry and the Catinet, this is a very distressed Esso, Ambassador to the High Peak. Larry, a DISASTER has happened. Second Employee says she doesn't want to be employed by Ghost and I any more and has 'completely had it with cats' and doesn't love us even a tiny little bit, even though she and I are special best friends and I have taught her the correct response in Cat when I call out 'I, Esso, am underneath the piano and all is well'. Larry, how can she have forgotten all our happy times? She says she is done, and isn't spending any more of her life 'wandering about being followed everywhere by cats like a mad person with Familiars when I used to be edgy and cool'. When was she edgy and cool, Larry?! Ghost and I certainly can't remember! And, yes, Ghost *does* have a current Witchcraft Familiar Licence (Novice Level), but at the moment she is non-practicing, and Second Employee knows that! So that is a really unfair thing to say about the familiars wandering about!

Larry, I have *absolutely no idea* what has precipitated this terrible resolution from Second Employee, but it all happened last night. Second Employee had come home late, after jumping up and down on a tiny trampoline in a church hall. Ghost and I were outside, keeping an eye on things. It was a beautiful evening. I had a nice chat with a Jackdaw, and we both agreed entirely independently, and without there being any undue pressure on anyone and with both parties being completely cognisant of the risks (albeit almost entirely theoretical) posed by my teeth, to continue our discussion inside the Embassy. However, when we got inside I remembered I had something to say to Grey Next Door Cat, and so I left the Jackdaw for a moment while I wrapped up a few loose ends. I do feel, deprived of my reassuring presence, he may have begun to feel a little anxious, even though I had assured him I would only be a moment: and he may possibly have begun to fly rather frantically up and down the hallway outside the living room, with quite a lot of flapping and squawking. These things, as you know, Larry, are just part of the cut and thrust of Embassy diplomacy, and there's no need for anyone to be *silly* about them: but the next thing we heard was Second Employee coming into the hallway, SCREAMING and SCREAMING, and then going back into the living room and slamming the door. Ghost crept up the stairs and listened outside, in case we needed to intervene, because of course we had no clue what on earth could be wrong: and she heard Second Employee on the phone, shouting, Keith, pick your bloody phone up, come home immediately you get this message, I'm trapped in the living room and it's terrifying, it's like a horror film. Well, Larry, obviously this was very very silly. What could she have meant?

Luckily, First Employee came home coincidentally very soon after that, and, also completely coincidentally and not because of anything that had happened up to that point, suggested to the Jackdaw that he might be happier outside: which did at least make everything a little quieter without all that FLAPPING. Ghost, though, said she had really heard terror in Second Employee's voice; and, although however hard we thought about it we couldn't work out what her problem was, she still felt sorry for her, because we are excellent Employers!

Ghost, as you know, is not given to generous impulses: so when she suggested going out to get a lovely present for Second Employee to cheer her up, I encouraged her very strongly. When Second Employee was in the basement later making 'a very strong coffee and I wish it was gin' even though she had got to go to bed in less than twenty minutes, Ghost strode through the cat flap with a live mouse in her mouth, trotted right up to Second Employee, and dropped it on her foot. Ghost thought playing with it for five minutes before bed would calm her down: but, alas, Larry, Second Employee was too stressed about whatever it is she was stressed about for even such a lovely distraction as this. She SCREAMED again, and this is when she said the terrible things about no more cats and being edgy and cool, which I still think is not true. So, Larry, could you intervene please? Ghost and I have decided that even though Second Employee has rejected our gift and hurt our feelings for utterly unknowable reasons which are probably linked to her own Stress or Low Self Esteem, we are willing to let bygones be bygones and allow her to continue as our Employee if she stops with her Silliness. Could you make Second Employee love us again, please, Larry?

June 2022

Larry, this is Ghost, Ambassador to the High Peak, here with a proper, sensible update after Esso FAFFING and FRETTING and MOPING in the last one. You'll be pleased to hear I've sorted everything out. I've pointed out to Second Employee that, whether or not she thinks she was cool and edgy for three days in 2003, or for those six days in 2015 when she could fit into her eBay biker jacket, I *personally* witnessed her the weekend before last making gooseberry jam and singing along to Gilbert and Sullivan Patter Songs: and no-one can be edgy who makes their own preserves and knows all the words to Am I Alone And Unobserved. Frankly, Larry, we are all embarrassed for Second Employee, and I am almost more embarrassed for Second Employee than I am for Esso, getting too attached to Employees and worrying whether they love him and following them about everywhere in a way that could look Needy to a cynical observer. Like me. So I said all this to Second Employee as we watered the garden together. I make sure Second Employee never goes out in the garden without me supervising her. I match her step for step. Anyway, everyone knows that Second Employee loves me best, because she says I am her special precious cat, and the softest creature in the whole of the High Peak; which as I have observed before, must be based on a significant collection of data, rigorously analysed. It is comforting to me, whenever I see Second Employee wandering about in her dungarees and Aldi Faux-Crocs looking rather unrigorous, that she at least in that instance must have followed a proper scientific method.

Now, I also have to report that Second Employee has made an Inappropriate Request, but you can be assured I quashed it immediately. She has told me that Esso's last update 'came up on First Employee's Facebook' which she 'had not realised could happen', and she said 'could I just be quite careful in what I say about people'. What remained unspoken, Larry, was the fact that First Employee combines a Shocking Level of

Nosiness with an equally shocking Lack of Discretion, and I understand Second Employee's concern. I am, though, unable to let issues of this nature stop me from reporting the Unvarnished Truth: because, as everyone knows, I cannot be trammelled. I shall also observe, Larry, that if my very useful and well-observed updates do 'come up on First Employee's Facebook' then that will set a very good example to him of the kind of Intellectual Precision and Gracious Living that both of the employees should be aspiring to: and it may also give everyone a break, however brief, from his sharing of all the most miserable articles in the Guardian about Brexit and Energy Bills.

Finally, I have a Diplomatic Success by Esso and I to report which is our success by us specifically. Interim Summer Employee has, as Second Employee's Mother has put it, 'successfully made the transition from the South to the North' and has moved to Buxton. This is solely because Esso and I have made it look interesting. We are very proud of ourselves. It is certainly not because of anything First Employee has said, because he is always moaning about the weather and telling people about a cricket match in Buxton one June being cancelled because of snow, and also about the time someone in the shopping centre was so horrified by his accent that they turned round to JUDGE him and walked slap bang into a pillar. Esso and I, however, are very aware of the possible culture shock and, indeed, necessity of adjusting to altitude when moving from the South to the North: after all, we both came all the way from Chesterfield Cats' Protection. What a journey that was! Esso is still working on the ballad. So we will be sure to keep a close eye on the Moral Development of Interim Summer Employee and try to make his adjustment as un-traumatic as possible!

I imagine you will be very impressed with our various successes, Larry, particularly with mine. Remember, I'm still in the market for that transfer to Derbyshire Dales!

July 2022

Larry and the Catinet: as you can see, it is Ghost, Ambassador to the High Peak, and I am having to do the update AGAIN because it is far too sensitive and important to leave to Esso and his FAFFING. Larry: Esso and I have been discussing the Second Employee Question, and we think we might have a solution. As I'm sure you can imagine, this is critical at the moment. July is the busiest month of the year in Buxton, with an Opera Festival, a Fringe Festival, a Gilbert and Sullivan Festival, a Carnival, a Well Dressing and all sorts of things. We are expecting lots of visitors, both to Buxton and to the Embassy: we need to make an excellent impression, and to do this we need Employees who are charming, urbane, cultured, intelligent, and not wandering round the garden barefoot, eating a biscuit, wondering aloud if they have planted too many salad leaves (yes they have). Larry, we have done our best to civilise

Second Employee, but it has become clear over the weekend, to me at least, that things cannot continue.

I shall give you an example of her Gauche Behaviour. A visitor came to stay with us this weekend, and the Employees took him to a very silly place in Matlock where you go up a mountain on a cable car and then go down into a cavern, despite there being a perfectly serviceable Buxton cavern just 20 minutes away from the Embassy which has the benefit of vastly superior Stalagmites. No matter. It was clear, when they returned, that Second Employee had let both herself and us down. Second Employee is claustrophobic, and is also terrified of heights: she had trotted into the cable car under the naive illusion that she would be absolutely fine, but it had 'randomly stopped mid-air' (I doubt, Larry, that it was truly random) and she had ended up crouched in a corner with First Employee's anorak over her head shouting 'don't take any notice of me, I'm not going to make a scene' to their Visitor, and to the nervous tourists who were sharing their car. Larry, how could she have made more of a scene? It is difficult to imagine. I suppose she could have climbed out of the car and caused a Fuss, but she and I both know she doesn't have the upper-body strength to Dangle for long periods!

[Note from Ghost: Second Employee has recently taken up Aerial Hoop, where she DANGLES from a suitably reinforced HOOP in a room on Hasland Trading Estate with a lot of other

Employees who have not managed to retain the sense they were born with. Not only is it very silly and quite pointless, but may mean she actually does have the upper body strength now to make climbing out of cable cars in a panic a possibility. I shall monitor her cable-car related activity very carefully if there is a chance she is now Strong Enough To Cause Trouble.]

Then, when I discussed the issue with Esso, we remembered the terrible time during the last festival, where Second Employee did not read the description of a Fringe Performance properly, and took First Employee and her Parents to see a performance poet whose poems were *completely and entirely* about Terribly Inappropriate Subjects. To compound Second Employee's error, because the audience was small, she, First Employee and her Parents ended up on the front row, which led to Second Employee's mother being less than three feet from a man very loudly performing a (surprisingly protracted) ballad about Premature Ejaculation. I think it is fair to say that Second Employee's mother did not enjoy this, and has not forgotten: although her father had fun, because he had forgotten to turn his hearing aids on, an omission which Second Employee's Mother strongly discouraged him from correcting until after the performance.

Larry: I am sure you will agree with me that for us to attempt the 2022 Season with Second Employee in tow will be social death. The problem, of course, is Esso: he says Second

Employee is his Top Best Friend, and when he came rushing through the cat flap five times this morning while she was having breakfast to tell her that is was still windy 'she was interested every time. You can't recruit a bond like that, Ghost'. I even confess to a certain fondness myself: but it doesn't mean she is suitable for all situations! Could you send us, please, Larry, an Interim Festival Employee. Not Interim Summer Employee, because I would not trust him not to laugh at Inappropriate Poetry, or indeed to write it. Someone entirely different, who wears structured clothing, and makes intelligent conversation and wise performance choices. Thank you, Larry. The Festival starts tomorrow, but if you could get someone to us before Sunday that would be ideal, as otherwise Second Employee will be going UNSUPERVISED to a Festival Mass and then an Opera, and who knows what embarrassing things she will do! In fact, I will ask Esso to check she won't be sitting in the Upper Circle where it is cheap, because I have said many times that it is only a matter of time before she drops her packet of Minstrels on someone in the Stalls below!

July 2022

Larry, this is Esso, Ambassador to the High Peak. Larry: I know you're having a few issues with your own staff being RIDICULOUS. I can't tell you how much I sympathise. It's just that I'm having a slight issue here too, though, and I wondered if I could consult you on something. I think if we could keep this between ourselves for the moment until we can establish that it really is just a minor administrative matter that no-one would ever worry about or check like Ghost says it definitely is, that would be great.

This is the issue: as you know (because you signed off her last CPD points when she went on that *Signs, Portents and How Your Employees Are Too Dim To Recognise Them* morning with Next Door Grey Cat), Ghost has her Familiar's Licence, but she is non-practising. This is a very important distinction. To change her licence to practising we would have to allocate her as a Familiar to a specific person, and the only Employee who's got any chance of filling in all the paperwork is First Employee, because he has lists and beepy things on his phone and is good at things like that; whereas Second Employee forgets and wanders off and 'feels oppressed' when she has to meet a deadline. So I have been absolutely clear with Ghost that if she's going to start practising it has to be with First Employee and we need all the forms signed off correctly in advance. Well, Larry, you can imagine what Ghost thinks about this, because she's PERVERSE: and she says, Esso, how do you think people have been managing having Familiars for thousands of years. Do you think they were all getting everyone to sign Form 221A and tick the disclaimer box saying they'd understood the terms and conditions. Well, Larry, yes I do think that, because we all know there were versions of Form 221A even with the Ancient

Egyptians, even if they were on Papyrus or the Hair Side Of Manuscripts: but Ghost *will not be said*.

I told her this and she was most unhelpful, Larry. She said, Esso, when I took up this post at the Embassy I gave up every dream I ever had, and they were all really reasonable dreams, not silly ones. I gave up the dream of a Bungalow in Derbyshire Dales or in the Hope Valley where the weather is not mad, the ground is Gently Undulating rather than Utterly Precipitous, and I would not have to climb four flights of stairs to get to my radiator. I gave up the dream of efficient Employees in structured clothes, talking about sensible subjects in quiet voices. I gave up the dream of cool sophistication and Ammonite-painted interiors, and drawers you could open without there being wool inside. And now that I am here, trapped up a mountain with A Loud Talkative Person and some half-cocked Kaffe Fassett, waiting for the annual eight months of snow to begin in August, you are expecting me to give up the one skill that could at least make things a little bit more efficient. Is that what you're saying, Esso? Well, Larry, of course I had to confirm that it was: and Ghost shouted well then Esso I'm an emotional dry husk with nothing left, and you have caused that, you have made me a husk, Esso, so I'm going to go and sit on your blanket and wait for the end times. Which she did. Which is not ideal, but not to worry! Everything is fine!

It's just that, Larry, since we had this conversation, I've noticed some things working a bit differently. Just one or two things. For instance, Second Employee can't grow a dandelion without killing it, but now we've got so many plants the Embassy looks quite alarming, and we can't let visitors leave without giving them salad leaves because of the Rocket Glut: I'm genuinely concerned about the courgettes. But most worryingly, Larry, Second Employee has managed to get a good set on her Strawberry Jam, and this is utterly unprecedented, because Second Employee is so confused by Pectin that she had to reframe her last batch as 'Strawberry Syrup' and give most of it to her mother 'to put on ice cream'. Ghost says Second Employee has just accepted she needs a strong Rolling Boil; but, Larry, I really think Second Employee's Strawberry Jam would not have set without some form of intervention, and I am asking myself what that intervention might have been. And I am looking sideways at Ghost while I ask. So, Larry, could I ask you, without me having said anything at all that would imply anything, what the penalty would be for a non-practising Familiar who might be Practising Secretly, and if perhaps there are forms which could be filled in retrospectively which might sort things out? Many thanks! And sympathies again for your own travails. My only advice is to try to get your Employees to stick to the Strategic Plan, but I know how often one looks at the Strategic Plan, then looks at the Employees, and despairs...

July 2022

[Note from Ghost: this was during the two days when temperatures in the high thirties were recorded in the High Peak, which caused near-panic in the local population. The local weather station, Buxton Weather Watch, advised us all in the fortnight leading up to it to do complicated manoeuvres involving opening and closing curtains and windows at very specific times and to drink copious amounts of fluids. Esso and I enjoyed the nice weather. Honestly, it made a change.]

Larry and the Catinet, this is Ghost, Ambassador to the High Peak. Larry, we've finally got some nice weather here in Buxton, but I wonder if we ought to notify the Catinet just to keep an eye on their Employees. As you know, Employees aren't desert-descended creatures like we are, and they don't always do too well in the heat. Esso and I have made sure Second Employee has a cool place to sit, and cold drinks available: but even so, she's doing quite a lot of drooping and googling the weather forecast to see if it's magically going to get a lot colder soon. Well, it is! So there's no need for Second Employee to stagger about fanning herself like some silly Victorian maiden although, as Esso points out, if she was actually a Victorian maiden she'd have to eat quite a lot less CAKE to get into her corset. I don't know, Larry, the DRAMA. Just because she's had to take her cardigan off for two days running and watch First Employee striding about saying, isn't this weather fantastic, Susie, let's move to the house in Spain next week so we can BASK in 39 degrees for 4 months of the year, she's gone into a decline. I know she's not herself, because yesterday she became unhelpfully obsessed with my Tiny Precious White Earsies, and then today she's been chasing Esso round trying to pull the seeds and burrs out of his fur, since he very sensibly spent most of last night under a bush. I'm sure everyone else's Employees are being much more professional, but remember, just check in on them occasionally to make sure they've got access to a shady place! Esso and I are going to have a little break this afternoon and do some BASKING of our own, but tomorrow we're going to do a major rewriting of the High Peak Embassy Strategic Plan 22-23. Yes, it's finally time for us to force Second Employee to fulfil those Key Performance Indicators!

July 2022

Larry, this is Esso here, Ambassador to the High Peak, with my update. Actually, Larry, as a very special concession to Second Employee which will of course not be repeated, I am allowing her to influence tonight's update, because she has something she would like to communicate to other Employees. We have agreed we will not tell Ghost, because strictly speaking we are aware that this contravenes protocol, and Ghost is very much a stickler for protocol; indeed, she has spent the last week knocking all the courgette flowers off the courgettes because

TECHNICALLY they are infringing the allocated courgette-free space by fifteen millimetres.

Anyway. Second Employee has a problem. A while ago, in response to fuel prices quadrupling and Organic Porridge Oats in Aldi going up to £1.69 which made them think the end of civilisation was just round the corner, the Employees decided they would economise by no longer hanging about in cafes drinking coffee and eating CAKE, but would invite their friends and family to the Embassy instead, where cake could be made very cheaply with the assistance of the Be-Ro book. Predictably, Larry, Second Employee has been a victim of her own success; just like when her brother became overwhelmed with demand for his Hyper-Realist Fried Egg Paintings and ended up with a flat full of enormous ones at different stages of completion, which was quite oppressive for visitors. With encouragement and support from Ghost, First Employee, and I, Second Employee has been just about keeping up with the Cake and Coffee Demand: however, now she has gone too far.

Larry, it is sad to see an Employee crumble under the weight of her own Silly Ideas. She has organised a Tea for her Parents' Golden Anniversary, and decided that she would make a Celebration Cake, which would be a rainbow cake covered in Buttercream with a Sparkly Topper, because her mother has always thought Rainbow Cakes 'look fun'. Larry, Second Employee has spent all week making Victoria Sponges in increasingly appalling colours, and stashing them in the freezer, and she would like other Employees to know that it is 'the stupidest idea she has ever had' because 'the entire thing looks unspeakable and hideous': and she suggests that they make sure they never do the same, but, 'buy a bloody Colin the Caterpillar and be done with it'.

I cannot approve of Second Employee's language, Larry, although I understand her despair. Ghost and I have looked in horror at what has come out of that oven over the last few days: and although it is perhaps conceivable that someone might be able to force down the orange layer, we really do not think anyone is going to be able to eat the green. And as for the purple - oh my goodness. It is fair to say, Larry, that we have never seen a colour quite like it. We do not know how Second Employee has managed to produce it, although, as Ghost says, we should have taken swift firm action before any of this started when we discovered Second Employee googling 'do gel food colours ever go out of date'. We have not dared to google this ourselves, Larry: we can only pray that the answer is no, because if Second Employee *actually* poisons everyone rather than her cake merely *resembling* toxic waste then that would be terrible. Terrible. Ghost says, on the bright side, if Second Employee 'takes her entire family out with that awful cake, Esso, it will at least stop them all talking about that time you bit her father'; and, perhaps a little selfishly, I can see the wisdom of this. But I feel, as a responsible Employer, I must hope that the rainbow cake does not actually poison anyone, and that Second Employee stays calm and sane enough to finish it and to serve it to them.

Larry, I think there are a number of lessons we should take from this. Firstly, I will ask Ghost to update the Risk Register to add the risks of Employees becoming unhealthily obsessed with baking inappropriate items: and I would like the Catinet, if possible, to warn their Employees to restrict Cake Making to no more than two layers, using only colours that are found in nature. I think that will eliminate the most egregious examples. Second Employee has set aside Friday for her crumb coat and for making 'a nice pink ganache to use as a drip': I forsee a number of issues with this, Larry. I really do. I hope you and the Catinet will think of us on Friday and through the weekend to come, because I do think this situation might necessitate a level of tact which is certainly beyond Ghost and may even be beyond me!

July 2022

Larry and the Catinet: this is Esso here, Ambassador to the High Peak, with, I am afraid, a Cautionary Tale. Larry, I updated only recently about Second Employee's ridiculous rainbow cake she had decided to make for her parents' Golden Anniversary. The Catinet were kind enough to sympathise with the trouble this was causing Ghost and I, and to warn Second

Employee about the brightly-coloured bowel movements which might ensue. [Note from Esso: I was very struck by the strength of the warnings from Catinet Employees about Bowel Movements. It concerned me greatly.] I am afraid that, despite my entreaties, Second Employee refused to warn her family explicitly about possible bowel movement issues as she handed them the cake, as I suggested. She said it would be 'offputting'. Offputting! Well, on her head be it. Anyway, this is just a brief update to let the Catinet know that Second Employee did manage to produce a Rainbow Cake, which, completely unaccountably, Second Employee's Mother in particular liked very much; despite not having herself purchased or produced anything which wasn't beige since approximately 1993.

I was hopeful, Larry, that we would manage to get the cake consumed and mostly out of the house without incident. However; it was not to be. Second Employee had refused to eat any of it at the specified time because she was 'getting over a migraine', so, when everyone had shared it upstairs in the sitting room, she took it down to the kitchen to portion out what was left for her family members to take home, and kept a small portion, upright on the cake stand, to save for later for her and First Employee. Unfortunately, while she was doing this, Ghost had jumped onto the table that the cake had been served on, and, as she explained to me before she fell into a drugged sleep, just decided to try 'a lick of buttercream and a few sprinkles to see what all that Godawful fuss had been about'. Well, Larry, one taste, and that was the end of it. Ghost says she doesn't remember clearly what happened next, just a few vivid snapshots, like a film: voices saying, look at that cat licking the table and pushing that sprinkle round with her nose: Second Employee coming back upstairs to see if anyone wanted YET ANOTHER cup of tea: running rather erratically off the table and down to the kitchen: the discovery of the leftover cake on the counter: a FRENZY of licking, a burst of over-enthusiasm, the cake skidding across the kitchen floor, the catflap: then the relative peace of the garden.

Well, after Ghost's Secret Orgy of Gluttony, Second Employee and Second Employee's Mother went downstairs to put the kettle on AGAIN, and everyone heard Second Employee shouting at the discovery of the cake in the middle of the kitchen floor, and Second Employee's Mother saying, *I bet that was Ghost*! I will not say anything about Second Employee's Mother *always being there to point the finger* whenever Ambassadors do anything Experimental, but; I am thinking it. Larry, selfishly, I do hope Second Employee's Family can now FINALLY move on from my teeth <u>once</u> - <u>once</u>! biting Second Employee's Father, and remember instead Ghost and her Buttercream Addiction!

Luckily, all has ended well. Second Employee picked the cake up, decided it was unharmed, and put it in a tin, saying, that floor is very clean. That may be true, Larry, or it may not be true: you and I would probably agree on the correct answer. Ghost is in the guest room sleeping off her indiscretions, having confessed to me before she fell asleep, which I imagine she will not remember. I am hoping when she wakes she will have forgotten her craving, and that we are not now in a terrible Goblin Market kind of situation. I will keep a very close eye on things. Second Employee says she never wants to see buttercream ever again. I think it is best for us all, Larry, especially Ghost, if she doesn't!

August 2022

Larry and the Catinet, this is Ghost here, Ambassador to the High Peak. Larry, you find me in pensive mood. Since I last updated, I have had to deal with a fairly serious Addiction Issue in one of the Employees. It is lucky, Larry, that at least one of we Ambassadors has read and {cough} *understood* the Dealing With Substance Abuse in Diplomatic Employees Policy 22-23 due for review in November and not a moment before time! Larry, you know I never, ever like to criticise Esso's way of working which is sometimes very different to mine and not as good. I will just say that every single hour I have put into almost tireless monitoring of BIRDY activity this year has been matched by Esso flopping pointlessly about on the rug or on his blanket, tapping Second Employee with his FEETIES to try and tempt her to grab them, or 'monitoring KPIs' by nuzzling her with his head and purring. And I think you and I are probably both very, very clear about whose contribution to the Overall High Peak Embassy Strategic Plan has been more valuable.

Anyway, I sat Esso down underneath Graham next door's bush which is much better trimmed than ours is which I have noted for future workplanning purposes, and I said, Esso, I need to talk to you about Addiction. Well, Larry, Esso is so preoccupied with his blanket and with whether or not Second Employee still loves him that he got the wrong end of the stick twice before we got anywhere at all constructive. First he said, oh God Ghost, I knew it. I knew one taste of buttercream wouldn't be enough for you. Well look, First Employee has banned Second Employee from making any more cakes for the moment because 'they are like crack', so if you can be brave and try and take it one day at a time, I'm sure we can get you through this. I'll ask Grey Next Door Cat if there are any local Buttercream Anonymous meetings you can attend. I think that Lightwood Road Hairy Siamese had a bit of a Nip thing going at one point and so they started a North Buxton chapter, perhaps you could jump in on that?

Well, Larry, obviously this was complete nonsense. I literally don't even know what Esso was referring to, unless it was a very, very minor incident the other weekend which was really too minor for anyone to notice at all, so if he was referring to this, perhaps you could ask him to stop referring to it immediately and never refer to it again. So I dismissed this very firmly and said, no Esso, OBVIOUSLY not me. Then he said, oh no, is it First Employee? Well, I'm not surprised, are you, Ghost? Not with everything we've heard about his Whirl of Gin and Decadence in Andalucia, living just like Marcus in Eldorado except in a much more inconvenient house right at the top of a mountain and with less money. That clearly wasn't going to last, was it Ghost, pretending he's happy sitting in Pavilion Gardens drinking coffee with Second Employee and thinking he's having a racy evening if they go to see one of the lesser-performed Gilbert and Sullivan Operettas, although Second Employee did say Utopia Ltd was actually much more exciting than I am giving it credit for.

Well Larry, I had to correct Esso again, because it is not First Employee, me, Grey Cat Next Door, Lightwood Road Hairy Siamese, Interim Summer Employee, or the man who is coming in September to update our fusebox. No. It is Second Employee, who has managed to become addicted to radishes. Yes, Larry, to radishes. As ever, Larry, it started off small, with Second Employee suggesting, in a calm and apparently disinterested way, that they should occasionally add radishes to a salad 'for a bit of crunch'. It ended with her in Aldi in Chapel En Le Frith shoving locals out of the way to get her Radish Fix having had to breathe through her panic when she found they were sold out in Buxton Morrisons. I will merely pause, Larry, to remark that only Second Employee could become obsessed with something quite so unglamorous. But at my prompting, First Employee has Intervened, and now she is taking her Iron Tablets again, because as soon as her Radish Habit goes above two packets a week we know that she is anaemic and must take action. That is the cut off for a Radish Addiction, Larry: anything more than two packets a week. I don't know if we should add that important information to the Substance Abuse Policy. And I don't know what Second Employee would do without me looking out for her: she would be in a terrible state! But, I do have to keep her in good enough shape physically to at least keep dishing out the biscuits, even if I might question her usefulness generally!

August 2022

Larry. This is Esso, Ambassador to the High Peak, with my Very Serious and Indeed Rather Grim update. Well, Larry, I have had to practically stand over Second Employee to make her type today's update, because Ghost has made it *quite clear to her* what she thinks about matters, and now Second Employee thinks she is BETRAYING US and has gone into a decline. Again. And is feeling almost too guilty to type, although hopefully not too guilty to be dishing out the biscuits until Sunday lunchtime. Yes, Larry, the Employees are going off scruffing around Spain again for *three entire weeks* while Ghost and I subject Interim Summer Employee to an intensive training course to try to *finally* get him up to scratch as a Feline Diplomatic Service Employee; although, as Ghost very rightly observes, it is a little bit like trying to up-skill Second Employee: i.e. a very similar experience to nailing a jelly to a wall. Not that either Ghost or I have ever actually tried to nail a jelly to a wall - our attempts to open the cupboard with the toolbox in have so far been unsuccessful, although we remain hopeful - but I imagine if someone told Second Employee it was fashionable to have jellies nailed to walls she would arrange a number of them in the hallway.

Anyway, although Ghost is currently sulking under Graham Next Door's Bush and has said she really feels this time that her 'looking terribly poignant in the suitcase' manoeuvre is entirely morally justified and she is going to perform it with Vigour and Alacrity, I do feel she is being a little unfair. As we both know, Second Employee would never leave the sofa in the dining room if she wasn't required to: either to go to work, or because First Employee is making her go on holiday and enjoy herself, which she really is very bad at, and which cannot be fun for either of them.

Ghost says the whole thing is ridiculous, and First Employee could have easily found a wife who was a chatty extrovert like he is practically by any other means than whichever one he *actually* used to find Second Employee. Indeed he could have done it 'just by sitting on the 199 Buxton to Disley Skyline Bus and shouting': and, frankly, she doesn't know why he didn't. But Larry, who knows why Employees want to be Employed Together. It is a mystery. It is not as simple a matter as just reallocating them to more appropriate co-Employees, as Ghost says it is!

Anyway, I have told Second Employee that on her perambulations around Spain, when she finally ends up at First Employee's Very Inconvenient House Which Is Up A Terrifying Mountain And There Is Never Any Water And There Are Goats, we may still require her services to do an update. In this way, I have reassured her that she is not completely useless! Ghost says she is 'done with Second Employee and her shocking absenteeism' and is going to get Interim Summer Employee to type the updates, but Larry, it is difficult to get the Employees to type without reading the updates at all; and I would just like to maintain high standards of confidentiality until Interim Summer Employee has formally passed his Intensive Summer Training 2022.

So Second Employee has agreed that if they still have free WiFi at Pepa's Bar Los Tres Balcones, she will try to do her update from there while she is eating her Chocolate Y Churros. And as a quid pro quo, I have agreed that I will not allow Interim Summer Employee to become bitten by my teeth very deeply again, no matter how silly and careless and deliciously biteable he might be. So hopefully, Larry, we will all make the most of the next three weeks - Interim Summer Employee is particularly lucky to have such a wonderful opportunity - and then when the Employees are home we can start the preparations for the Happy Cold Times, which we understand are going to be particularly exciting and challenging this year!

August 2022

Larry and the Catinet; this is Esso, Ambassador to the High Peak. I understand that the Catinet have decided it would be instructive for our Employees to learn how we attained our roles so that they can perhaps be inspired to Better Themselves. Ghost said to me, go on Esso, tell them your origin story like Batman, but I ignored this Unsupportiveness and Disrespect.

Ghost and I were born in a flat in Chesterfield; and our first Employee had a number of interests, the main ones being collecting as many cats as possible, and taking Heroin. Sue, who was our friend from Chesterfield Cats' Protection, used to visit, and she persuaded him that the absolutely optimum number of cats for someone in his situation was, coincidentally, at least two fewer than he actually had. So Ghost and I volunteered to leave and go with Sue while we waited to see what the World had in Store: and so we found ourselves in Sue's garage, which was converted into temporary cat accommodation, much in the manner of AirBnB.

Then one day, Sue came and told us that Second Employee had contacted her by email! Obviously she was Unknown Employee then, but she had asked if Sue had a pair of cats and she 'didn't mind the age or the colour', and she was coming to visit us! Sue told us she had said that I was a bit of a biter and Ghost was a bit unfriendly, but, she could come and see if she liked the look of us, and, if she did, she could take us home. Well, Ghost was very cynical about this, especially when she learned that Second Employee was living in Buxton: so she said, look Esso, you bite her when she gets here and we'll hold out for someone hopefully with a bit more money and living in the Hope Valley. But I felt unsure. Larry, I am not prone to Unhelpful Thoughts: but I sat that night in our cat enclosure, and I looked around me at the concrete walls, and I thought about things. I thought about our first Employee and his interest in Heroin, and I thought about Ghost and I ending up all alone in a garage, and I thought of my mother's words: no one ever wants black cats, Esso. And then I thought of Unknown Employee (as was) coming to see us the next day and perhaps saying, these cats are too unfriendly and monochrome and bitey, I shall go back to Buxton and hold out for a Cuddly Ginger.

And then Ghost came to sit with me, and said, are you crying, Esso? Which of course I wasn't, it was just that my eyes sometimes run a little in Winter. So she said, would you feel better if you thought you had a Mission, because you like a

Mission, don't you? And I said, yes, perhaps, but we haven't got a Mission; we are just two quite small Kittens in a Garage, and tomorrow we are going to be rejected. So I could see Ghost thinking. And then she suddenly said, guess what, Esso. I forgot to tell you! Sue and I were talking earlier, and she said, we've been chosen to be the Catinet Ambassadors to the High Peak! It's a very important job - we've got to bring Gracious Living to the High Peak and get started on a Strategic Plan! Well, Larry, obviously this put an entirely different slant on the matter: I couldn't believe Ghost hadn't remembered earlier. I stayed up for the rest of the night working on the first draft of the Strategic Plan, and, the next day, First and Second Employee turned up with a cat carrier and put Ghost and I into it, no questions asked: because First Employee said, although he was sure there were people who could sensibly assess a pair of Kittens and deem them either suitable not suitable, there was no point in pretending Second Employee was one of them; so they had come prepared, and there were lots of sofas and blankets and a big bag of food back at the Embassy.

So that, Catinet, is how Ghost and I were chosen to be Ambassadors. I will only add to this that it was Ghost who did Second Employee's initial interview, and I do wish she had made her Job Description clearer: but no matter. I hope we have all tried to do our duty, albeit some of us a little more efficiently than others!

Chapter 7

Autumn 2022: Second Employee begins her long and interesting career of telling people to shove their JOBS right up their BUMS

September 2022

Larry this is Ghost here, Ambassador to the High Peak, with a VITALLY IMPORTANT and URGENT legislation request. Please prioritise this above all other things, Larry, I am going to need you to act quickly, because Esso has *only just* confessed to me about a Situation that is brewing. I have been saying to him, Larry, for the whole *ridiculously extended period* that the Employees have been away when there has been literally no-one to love or stroke me at all apart from Interim Summer Employee who does stroke me quite a lot but honestly I may as well go feral and that would serve everyone right), that I wonder what Second Employee is doing. Because obviously she will have a chart she has made of 'days until I see Ghost again' which she colours in daily, and she probably spends quite a bit of time arguing about the Mad House Up A Mountain with First Employee; but I cannot imagine that doing even both these things consecutively can take more than a couple of hours a day. So what else is she doing going scruffing all around Spain, and is it something that will make her a More Effective Employee. Ha! I doubt it!

Well, Esso has been saying to me all this time, he thinks she has probably been looking at all the gold leaf and religious iconography and amazing geometric tiles in the major Andalucian cities and thinking, actually, these are all a bit much and beige is better. Larry, of course this sounded wonderful: I believed my brother and Co-Ambassador implicitly. The thought of Second Employee being exposed to the cream of Iberian Maximalist Design and realising I was right all along! I have been thinking, I will get the Farrow and Ball Paint Chart out again when she comes back and indicate Ammonite with my nose, and perhaps FINALLY we can get the hall repainted to something sensible. Then today Esso came to talk to me with a guilty expression on his furry face, and told me that he had - and there is no nice way of putting this, Larry - been lying to me all along ('because you are so awkward and rigid, Ghost' - as if that justifies it!) and that *actually* he knew that Second Employee had been having *a high old time* wandering round the ceramics quarter of Seville buying all sorts of brightly-coloured horrors, and had - and this is the worst - visited a 'really good-value dealer in Moroccan furniture in quite a random industrial estate just outside of Malaga and bought a rather fun little painted table'.

Well, Larry, I have to draw the line somewhere: and I am drawing it at small brightly-painted Moroccan occasional tables sourced from artisans by dealers on Malagan industrial estates. I will *not have* such a thing in this house. I am revoking Second Employee's UK citizenship unless she leaves it on the ferry. Larry, there is still time for us to act: I understand from Esso, who is now, of course, singing like a canary, that the Employees are currently holed up in a hotel up a mountain in San Sebastian, in a room which is very high up and where they are too frightened to go out on to the balcony. I believe we have three nights' grace, as they are scheduled to arrive in Portsmouth at roughly 5:30pm UK time on Sunday evening. Could you, please, pass immediate emergency legislation to ban the import for personal use of the following: Moroccan painted anything: ridiculous ceramics which are not something like grey earthenware cereal bowls which would at least be useful: anything decorative which has not been pre-approved by Ambassadors (i.e. me, not Esso!).

Thank you, Larry. I am willing to have Second Employee back to stroke me if she does not bring a lot of Silly Things with her. I believe this legislation will be easier for you to pass post-Brexit: I suggested this to Esso, and he said, oh have you found a Brexit Benefit, Ghost, I shall tell the Telegraph to hold the front page. But, there is no need for Esso to be SARCASTIC, because this whole situation which has arisen is his fault to start with! I think it is now time, Larry, for the Employees to return, so that Second Employee can be aesthetically reprogrammed by me and spend the winter forgetting any Ridiculous Ideas she has got into her head over the last three weeks!

September 2022

Larry and the Catinet, this is Esso, a very worried Ambassador to the High Peak. Larry, I know you're going to have a lot on for the next few days trying to start your new Rescue Employee on her workplan - my advice is, establish KPI expectations early and don't ever expect them to show initiative, because they won't - but I just wanted to give you a quick update of how things are going here.

[Note from Esso: Ghost says I should mention that it was at this point that Larry was employing a lettuce. I do not know what Ghost means, but then I often don't, so I have chosen just to reproduce her words verbatim as she seems to think they are relevant to the preceding sentence.]

Well, it's all been a tiny bit difficult. I may have, completely inadvertently, very slightly misled Ghost about Second Employee's activities in Spain: I may, entirely without any design and not at all just wanting a quiet life, have implied that Second Employee was having an Aesthetic Renaissance whereby she was going to reappear and say, I have now had enough of bright colours, and am going to repaint the hall a subtle shade of greige. Of course, that was not actually true; so eventually I confessed to Ghost that she may have become only very slightly misled by some things I might possibly have unintentionally said or not said, for which I assume she takes full responsibility, because of course the responsibility is not mine. Very unfortunately, whoever's responsibility it was (it was Ghost's), she reacted very badly. The night before the Employees were due to get the ferry back, she tried to make me contact the Spanish Authorities to tell them that Second Employee was 'stashing drugs' in a small blue Moroccan occasional table I may possibly (although I don't entirely remember) have mentioned that the Employees had bought. Well, of course, I couldn't do that, because Second Employee is as likely to stash drugs as she is to give up cake for a week, so it seemed most unfair: also, imagine the administrative nightmare trying to get them out of prison! So I pretended I was doing what Ghost said via a 'report your Employee' function on the Spanish Government Website, but, in reality, I was talking to the Online Chat Bot on a website which sold sofas. In fact, I am a bit concerned I may have inadvertently ordered a bespoke four-seater in mustard velour.

Anyway, when the Employees appeared, I made a strategic decision to go outside and have a chat with Grey Next Door Cat about how we're dealing with a certain new interloper (long-haired black with a red collar and half a tail) - but, Larry, I needn't have worried, because Ghost forgot all about Second Employee and her Contraband by making a Holy Show of herself. Grey Cat and I heard quite a commotion, so I rushed back into the house to discover Ghost sitting looking a bit wide-eyed on the hallway carpet, and Second Employee stroking her and saying, listen to you miaowing away. Apparently, Second Employee had come back, rushed into the house to see if we were here, seen Ghost who completely ignored her as per Protocol 19B subsection 1492, and rushed out again, leaving the very heavy door very slightly ajar: Ghost had thought she was leaving again, and so had PUSHED the door open, run out into the street, and screamed at Second Employee: 'Come back Second Employee! Don't leave me again! I know I tried to have you arrested by the Guardia Civil, but I've had no-one to knead on properly and no-one to tell me how soft I am! Don't leave again! Come back! I LOVE YOU!'

Well, of course, Second Employee hadn't been leaving again at all, as Ghost would have realised if she had just thought about things for a moment: she had just been going back to the car to help First Employee with the suitcases. So now Ghost is MORTIFIED, and even more so as the Employees saw her trying out a new small rug they had brought back with them in the dark when she thought no-one was looking. I told Ghost I had looked at the label and it had been hand tufted by Iranian Nomads in the 1970s, but Ghost says that makes the whole situation worse, if such a thing is possible, and she cannot even retreat to her radiator because it is not cold enough yet to turn it on; especially as the Employees have just been offered a fixed-price deal of £996 a month, which we think may be slightly more than they have been used to paying. So Larry, it is all a bit difficult. I don't, honestly, know how Ghost can now recover face with Second Employee: all I can hope is that after twenty-six hours of being seasick on a ferry her comprehension of Cat was less than it usually is and she just heard a lot of very loud miaowing. I have decided it is best not to mention it again, and if anyone else mentions it, to pretend I haven't heard them. Dignity in public office is so important, isn't it, Larry, and we must always try to maintain it, no matter the personal cost!

September 2022

Larry, this is Ghost, Ambassador to the High Peak. Larry, I need to report a Disrespectful Thing that Esso has said to me. I was taking time out to recuperate after all my hard work with BIRDIES over the summer, and he said, look at you, Ghost, haven't you been relaxed since Second Employee has been back. Well, Larry, I DEEPLY resent the implication that I would notice in any way the fact that Second Employee left me all alone with no-one to love or stroke me at all for twenty one days, twenty two hours and thirty five minutes. I honestly barely noticed she was gone. As an unconnected aside, I have been checking her contract of employment, and I have realised our error: although Esso states very clearly in it that she has a contractual leave entitlement of twenty five days + bank holidays per year, he forgot to add 'pro rata'! So, since Second Employee only really does anything constructive for about twenty minutes a week, if you think how many twenty minutes there are in twenty five days she could be off all year! No wonder she has been confused and going wandering about in ridiculous places. She probably thinks she's contractually obliged to. She was probably sitting drinking coffee in Seville saying to First Employee, how I wish I was back at home telling Ghost how soft she is, but according to my contract I've got to stay here at least until I've bought all the ceramics in Triana, had a good look round the Cathedral, and eaten my body weight in tapas. It is actually very sad to think of Second Employee missing me like this when of course I did not miss her at all, not even a tiny bit. However, because I am a thoughtful Employer, I am going to reissue her contract immediately with that error corrected; and then she will realise it is best to stay here at all times, appreciating how soft and clever I am. So that is that situation sorted out.

Also, Larry, just as I had decided to contact Glossop Furniture Project and ask them to take away the silly new table, Esso has become attached to it, even though my colouring sets it off much better. He has taken to sitting underneath it, even though when you sit in that position you can see all Second Employee's less intellectual books which are on the bookcase behind. Obviously I don't judge, but I will *just say* that if she had read a bit less Jilly Cooper and a bit more Hilary Mantel she might be a marginally better Employee. Also, Larry, Second Employee has got another one of her silly 'jobs' she does out of the house [Note from Ghost: this ended badly] where she goes to stare at spreadsheets and say, I can't make it balance; which both Esso and I are amazed anyone pays her for, because *I also* could go and tell people there is not enough money, and I would do it without having to be given constant cups of coffee and fed biscuits which are 'anything except Rich Tea'.

Anyway, because it is a new job [Note from Ghost: and one, it turned out, of Short Duration], she has declared that at least for the first month she cannot wear her dungarees but must wear 'professional clothing'; so Esso and I have both been watching her with the cold eyes of judgement as she tries to make various cardigans fasten across her chest. What price all that cake now, Second Employee? But, if it is a new job, with new people who do not know her, why have Esso and I not been formally contacted for a reference? I have got a very instructive reference to give! I know Second Employee inside out, and she is quite unsuitable to be going getting jobs with strangers. Firstly I know that she is quite unable to put together a professional outfit, as I have seen her trying to cobble something together involving yoga leggings and a pentagram pendant; and also, she has got a very limited capacity for networking, which will probably be exhausted in the first half a day, and thereafter will retreat into sarcasm and looking at knitting patterns online in her lunch hour. Which is not the action of a modern, go-getting career woman, which I would certainly be if I had very slightly less fur and very slightly more opposable thumbs.

So, Larry, could you instruct whoever has been silly enough to employ Second Employee that they need to contact me asap so I can give them the proper lowdown, and could you also let Esso know that he is not to sit near the Silly Table when it has quite obviously been bought specially as a backdrop for me. Many thanks, Larry, and I can assure you that my resting has made me an even more dynamic Ambassador!

September 2022

Larry: this is a Cri De Coeur from a terribly, terribly sad and worried Esso, Joint Feline Ambassador to the High Peak. Larry, I am contacting you in confidence. I feel my position has become untenable, and I feel I have to be honest with you and, most of all, with myself, about the situation. I haven't been entirely honest with Ghost yet, obviously, because she really is quite a difficult cat, but with you I shall Speak My Truth.

Larry, I feel I must resign my post, and I shall explain to you how this has come about. Because of my and Ghost's excellent training, Interim Summer Employee has become very much in demand as an Interim Employee To Others, and in a few weeks is going to be employed temporarily by a large chunky cat called Archie whose Employees are going wandering off in Macchu Picchu and the Galapagos for a couple of weeks, which is even more ridiculous than Second Employee going scruffing round Seville. Indeed, thank goodness Second Employee didn't go to the Galapagos, because she would probably have come back with a Giant Souvenir Tortoise. It would probably be marching round the garden as we speak, intimidating Grey Next Door Cat, and with Ghost looking at it BEADILY from under the Ornamental Currant. Anyway, the Employees and Interim Summer Employee went to have lunch with Archie's current staff so his preferences could be explained, and Second Employee told me that Interim Summer Employee was explaining how well he has been trained by Ghost and I. But then, apparently, he told everyone that my teeth had bitten him quite deeply, and my claws had scratched him quite strongly, and then he laughed and said to Second Employee, well he is a bit of a biter, isn't he, he put your father in hospital. Larry! I did not! Second Employee's Father didn't go to hospital until at least a fortnight later, and no-one has ever proved that his *own actions* of becoming unhelpfully involved with my teeth were connected at all! And besides, he came out of hospital, and he is fine!

But Larry, I feel despair. How can I ever move on from the completely random and not at all malicious actions of my teeth when no-one will ever let me forget? I really feel that the inability of Second Employee's Social Connections to move on is making my position untenable. I voiced some of my concerns to Ghost, and she said, look, Esso, everybody is here in Buxton because they've got something they want everyone to forget about, or everyone would be living somewhere sensible where it doesn't rain every single day and you don't need crampons to get to Waitrose. Second Employee is here trying to pretend she didn't spend nineteen years in an abusive relationship and also wear a tutu to work with a straight face. And who knows what Bad Choices First Employee made, but you know the amount of gin he used to put away every week so I don't imagine he was doing all that and then playing Rummikubs. So all you have done differently, Esso, is waiting until you got to Buxton before you made your Bad Choices, if you had just bitten everyone in Chesterfield no-one would have known and it would all be forgotten by now.

Well, Larry, this has concentrated my mind and stiffened my resolve. Perhaps it is time for me to move on and become the Catinet Ambassador to Cheadle Hulme, or to somewhere even worse, like Stockport, and leave my Tooth-Based Travails behind. The one thing, Larry, that gives me pause is that Second Employee might miss me. My teeth haven't caused her any trouble yet - well, they've never quite broken her skin - and I don't think she really appreciates the Shame they have brought on my Dignified Role. Larry, I am unable to square this circle, and I await your advice. I believe the normal procedure when Ambassadors bring their roles into Disrepute is to promote them out of the way of trouble: perhaps Ghost and I should both have the transfer to Derbyshire Dales, although, without Second Employee I must confess that for me it will ring hollow. Perhaps it would be easier and more straightforward, Larry, for you to arrange for Second Employee's Family, particularly her mother, to 'forget' the teeth incident? I am sure this could be arranged. I think, on reflection, this would be my preferred solution. Can I leave it with you, Larry? I know you might be a little busy this week, so I do understand if you can't get to it until next Wednesday or so!

September 2022

Larry and the Catinet, this is Ghost, Ambassador to the High Peak, with a brief update. Larry, Esso has been RIDICULOUS this last couple of days, maundering about, rolling on his back on the spare room bed, sitting doing slow blinks at Second Employee, and muttering about what a hard life he has and Why Oh Why must his teeth be so recalcitrant. Well, Larry, I will tell you why Esso's teeth are so recalcitrant: it is because they are attached to Esso, and he uses them to bite people. And, annoyingly, while he is DROOPING all over the place and not taking the one action that would actually help matters - namely, *not biting people any more* - who is taking on ALL the mental load? Me.

Someone very silly has given the Employees a new chest of drawers, and Second Employee has been transferring all her THINGS into it, and I have had to supervise by touching everything with my nose and telling her what she has got to get rid of. For example, earlier today I was looking through a pile of 'random things she had found' on the bed, and saying, Second Employee, when did you last wear coral nail varnish because frankly I do not think it was even in this century; so I think it is time to move it on. Also, can you note that statement necklaces are out of fashion, and you will have to find some other way to make use of those lampwork beads; and is that chalk for pole dancing, because these days I think it will take you more than that to get up a pole, it will take crampons and a step ladder.

Larry, at least this time First Employee had warned the Men With The Van who were bringing the Silly Chest Of Drawers quite how many floors there are in this house, but only because Second Employee had put her foot down and said if she had to be the one to come home from work and supervise she was 'not having another situation like when the men from Ikea delivered the sofas'; because, Larry, they did look as if they had gone through the Valley Of The Shadow Of Death when they had to carry the one for the basement backwards down our Side Jitty and no-one has forgotten it, although the Oak Kitchen Dresser was apparently an even worse experience and Second Employee is still unable to talk about it. I don't know what work

Second Employee thinks she does anyway, frankly, Larry, that isn't stroking me.

Still, now the new Chest Of Drawers is all full up again and order has been restored, which is solely due to my efforts, I have said to Esso: the time for MAUNDERING is over. Second Employee has invited her family again for tea on Saturday and he has got one last chance to prove he can be in the same room as Visitors without Biting. And do you know what he said to me, Larry? He said *and you've got one last chance, Ghost, to prove you can be in the same room as Buttercream without Licking!* Larry, could you please stop Esso being ridiculous and unhelpful and remembering things that everyone has completely forgotten, and make him focus properly on the Strategic Plan!

September 2022

Larry, this is Esso, Ambassador to the High Peak, with my Update. Larry, it has all kicked off. Ghost is offended again. In fact, Larry, Ghost says she will not put up with this level of Disrespect, and she is considering her position re: putting in a formal complaint about Second Employee. It was all going so well, Larry. I was cuddling up to Oscar the owl, who the Employees once liberated from a Craft Market in St Ives: Ghost was pacing about upstairs, BROODING about the efficacy or not of Liz Truss's strategy for economic growth; First Employee was lounging about on one sofa, and Second Employee was looking at her laptop on the other. It was nice and warm, and out of the corner of my eye, I noticed Brian from next door wandering along in front of the fireplace and slipping behind the sofa.

Well, Larry, it's Ghost who has made friends with Brian, not me: she says, in her capacity as Non-Practicing Familiar it's expected of her to make friends with Enormous Spiders, and actually they bring good luck and money so she's going to invite them all into the house. First Employee met one of Brian's compatriots the other day, 'striding through the kitchen with Ghost, as bold as brass', and relocated him into the garden with the help of a glass and one of those recipe cards from Waitrose: and Ghost said to me, if she invites friends in, she is not having First Employee relocate them anywhere with Waitrose Recipe Cards, because this is far more her house than it is his, because she owns it and he is just an Employee.

[Note from Esso: after we initially circulated this update, a particularly Tricksy Employee notified us that if we looked into the Ownership of the Embassy we might be surprised. We did and we were HORRIFIED. But more later.]

So that is why Brian is staying here, to help Ghost make a point. Although, to be fair, he's a nice chap, and we were having a very interesting chat the other night about Trickle-Down Economics.

Anyway, we were all sitting together, companionably, with Brian sitting right next to Second Employee, looking over her shoulder at Facebook Marketplace, when suddenly she saw him, jumped up and SCREAMED: so of course I jumped up and ran away, Brian jumped up and ran away, and Ghost ran downstairs to see what was happening. Second Employee saw Ghost, and said, Ghost, there is a BLOODY ENORMOUS SPIDER in this house, aren't cats supposed to eat spiders, I suggest you read your Job Description better! Well, Larry, you can imagine.

Ghost says she will not be TRAMMELLED or DICTATED to, and has decided to go and live with Mrs Hinch because at least her house is entirely beige, and Second Employee can come and visit daily between the hours of five and seven to Do Stroking: which I have told her is no good, because it does not look to me from her Instagram Stories that Mrs Hinch lives anywhere near Buxton, and Second Employee really does not like motorway driving. Brian says he doesn't want to upset anyone, but he does think Second Employee needs keeping an eye on in terms of what she is buying on Facebook Marketplace, so he is going to stay for another month or so: and Second Employee says, as she always does, that she wants to live in a new-build flat with no stairs, spiders, cats, or anyone who is going to talk to her. Well, Larry, we cannot all have what we want. Second Employee cannot have a new-build flat with no-one bothering her: Ghost cannot go and live with Mrs Hinch, warm neutrals notwithstanding: and Brian will have to move in down the road instead if he is going to upset the balance of our happy household. Although his views on Keynsian Economic Theory really were very interesting, Larry! Never mind - I will be the bigger cat, and sacrifice my rights to Improving Conversation in the interests of family harmony!

October 2022

Larry and the Catinet, this is Ghost here, Ambassador to the High Peak, with a VITALLY IMPORTANT update. Larry, I have a terrible tale of either SKULDUGGERY or INCOMPETENCE to relate to you regarding the Employees. It is a shame, because I have been rather pleased with Second Employee recently. She has bought a rug for the bedroom which is the same colour as me. I approve of it very highly. She also says I 'set off bright colours really well when I walk past them' so she is going to introduce more white and black things. Well, Larry, trumpets sound and angels sing: it may be the dawnings of a Proper Aesthetic Sense for Second Employee. So I will not hear anything against her this week, although Esso did tell me he heard a Disrespectful Conversation the other night. He was asleep on his chair in the sitting room, and the Employees were watching the first series of the Crown which they have got into after everyone else has lost interest, as is their way, and worrying about Princess Margaret. Then, apropos of nothing because I can't imagine Princess Margaret ever had to engage with a Flymo, First Employee said to Second Employee, I don't think I really need to mow the lawn tomorrow, and Second Employee said, well Esso thinks you should. Of course, Larry, this is quite correct. Both Esso and I think that First Employee is just being lazy about the lawn and it needs one more go at it before the Snows Come. Anyway, First Employee replied, no he definitely doesn't think that, and anyway you can't use the cats to channel your ambivalent feelings about our relationship passive-aggressively, Susie, that is not what cats are for. So Second Employee said, well, what are cats for, then, because that is literally their function, and First Employee said, you know what our cats are for. Esso is for biting and Ghost is for judging. I walked into the room at this juncture, just to check that Second Employee wasn't doing anything I ought to disapprove of, and everyone laughed. So I am minded to disapprove of this conversation, but I did not hear it myself and only report what Esso said about the matter, and as you know, sometimes he is not listening properly, and is thinking of biscuits.

Anyway, this is taking me away from my Important Update. The other day, Larry, a rather disrespectful Employee called Rona replied to Esso's update to suggest to him that it was actually the Employees who own the Embassy legally, and not us. This concerned Esso greatly, and he and Brian the spider sat all that evening looking at the Land Registry online trying to work out what the situation is, luckily it turns out that Brian owns a small terrace of houses in Sutton In Ashfield and is very familiar with machinations around property. Now, Larry, this will astonish you: she was correct. The Employees own the Embassy as Joint Tenants, and Esso and I do not own it at all. We were horrified. Firstly, of course, we suspected Criminal Activity and Fraud: but then we both watched Second Employee standing in front of the open fridge door for quite a long time saying, I'm sure I've opened this for a reason, and we realised the Employees do not have the intellectual powers to have scammed us.

We think what must have happened is that they took on the official ownership of the Embassy when they were employed, in order to set things up before Esso and I began our official roles, and have either neglected or forgotten to transfer the ownership to us. This can be easily remedied, Larry, I am sure, but at the moment we are in a slightly perilous position: as you know, Employees come and go. How many have you had now? So to protect Esso and I, in case we face a similar situation, we are going to instruct a local solicitor to transfer the ownership to us. I shall let you know how we get on. In the meantime, other members of the Catinet may wish to check who is named on their tenancy agreement, mortgage, deeds, or whatever paperwork - you may have a shock like us! Luckily, we are all now warned, and can take steps to make sure our Employees have no security of tenure whatsoever!

October 2022

Larry and the Catinet, this is Ghost, Ambassador to the High Peak, with my update on how silly Second Employee is being. Well, Larry, Second Employee is now working in two different jobs and is very confused, and every morning when she gets up First Employee says to her, where are you going today, and she has to think about it carefully. Second Employee says she has managed to get herself into a situation where she is dealing with two different audits at the same time, and how has that happened; and in the new job she has to use Sage and she is not intellectually capable, especially given that it took her three weeks to work out where the light switch in the toilet was and even then she had to ask her colleague to demonstrate. She says her only comfort is that she started her new job at the same time as Liz Truss started hers, and so far she is just about going down better with her new colleagues than Liz is with hers, although it is a close thing.
Well, Larry, obviously Second Employee is going to crash and burn very quickly, [Note from Ghost: I spoke here as a prophet] so this is all academic: and, when she does, I shall merely look at her with my particular expression: but, in the meantime, it makes no odds to Esso and I. We spend all morning before she leaves chasing her round the house, then sleep all day so we

are ready to chase her round again as soon as she comes in in the evening. She says she doesn't understand how, as a Confirmed Introvert (which, Larry, I think is another way of saying Very Silly Person), she has ended up with two different jobs where she has to talk to people all day, married to a Very Chatty Person, and with cats who follow her around everywhere. Second Employee says her original plan for her life, many many years ago, was to become an Academic in an Ivory Tower working on something very detailed and obscure, and to never have to speak to anyone: but it began going wrong when she took against one of her tutors because she didn't like the style of her trousers, although now she sees that was a bit shallow.

Well, Larry, I hardly think there is anything Second Employee would have had to say about Obscure Texts that the world has missed out on, and besides, we don't follow her around everywhere *at all*. That is *quite* untrue. I just have to check what she is doing! For instance, this morning, she was making soap, even though a sensible Employee would buy it from a shop; so obviously I had to make sure she was making it correctly even though she kept saying, Ghostycat, please don't put your nose in the lye solution. Larry, could you issue a memo please to emphasise that Ambassadors should put their Nosies in just as much Lye Solution as they want to, although I will ask Esso just to check first that it is not caustic: because we did write into the Strategic Plan the need to Check Substances Before Not

After, after that time Esso walked across the porch floor when Second Employee had just painted it and had Yves Klein Blue Feeties for a whole week.

But, Larry, this is not the worst I have got to report today. No. At her new job, Second Employee has managed to appoint someone who has a Terrible Incapacitating Fear Of Cats. Larry, how has she done this? I sometimes feel there is no limit to the ways Employees and Reluctant Potential Employees find of being Ridiculous. Second Employee says the new person, despite being generally robust, is so terrified of cats that when she saw one in her garden she was unable to leave the house until it was gone: and later, when she was finally able to go outside, she told her neighbour of her dreadful experience: and her neighbour said she was a 'big girl's blouse'. Second Employee says she advised her that cats are 'a little bit scary tbh', and that you have to think of them, rather than as pets, as 'small furry demons who are living in the house with you'. Larry, Esso and I are not sure how to react to this. Obviously it is true: but we feel it is disrespectful, and would not make anyone less frightened: but then again, obviously it is true, and rather well observed. So we are going to have a meeting later to consider the issue. In the meantime, Larry, I would like to ask you, who on earth uses the phrase Big Girl's Blouse unironically in 2022, and how has Second Employee, once again, found herself living in a Dick Emery sketch? It is all very silly. Anyway, I shall go and attempt to organise the Employees to be generally better people, Larry, and I will update again when I have finally made some progress!

October 2022

Larry, and the Catinet. This is Esso, Ambassador to the High Peak, with a very important update. Oh, goodness, Larry, it has been quite a week, and I'm afraid to say that Ghost is upset again. I don't wish to be disloyal, Larry, but I do very occasionally have the uncharitable thought that Ghost is a little bit prone to making things all about herself, but then of course I suppress it.

Last night I sat carefully on a hat in the shape of a fish which Second Employee is knitting for Christmas for Geoff, her brother in law. Ghost and I are a little confused why she is doing this, I must confess: we thought she liked Geoff. He doesn't enjoy fishing, either, as far as we know. Second Employee says that *actually* he enjoys golf, but, this is the pattern she has got and it is for a fish hat not a golf hat and everyone will have to deal with it, because she is saving money on presents now she has given up her job. Yes, Larry, Second Employee has been causing trouble again. She has resigned from one of her jobs. She lasted four days. Second Employee says her only regret is not walking out after the first day because it would have made a better anecdote, but, at least now she has got time to make that 'bloody green tomato chutney'.

Apparently things were said about Trial Balances which could not be unsaid, and Second Employee took PROFOUND UMBRAGE. Second Employee says she has not had an experience like that since many years ago, when she fell out with the Bursar in a Cambridge College [Note from Esso: the careful reader at this point may begin to see a pattern] she had found herself working in temporarily, and he would only communicate with her by hiding behind the door until she had gone to the toilet and then leaving notes on her chair. Larry, of course on one level I am deeply ashamed that, despite the HOURS Ghost and I have put into Employee Development, Second Employee wasn't even able to last as long in her new job as Kwasi Kwarteng did in his: but on the other level of course it is all much better, because now Second Employee is around much more and we are getting some really productive stroking (her) and purring (me) done. So I am very happy.

Ghost, of course was annoyed, and said, look Esso, clearly Second Employee is a flaky Employee, as I have always said; so we must get out her contract and look at it, because it's possible we never formally confirmed her probation, and if that's the case we could extend it for another six months with a view to managing her out. Well, Larry, I had to be honest. I said, look Ghost, it might not be a case of us extending Second Employee's probation. She might have tasted blood! She might resign from us next, and what will you do then? I've always suspected her of having slightly anarchistic tendencies. What if she says to you, Ghost, I am DONE with you following me around looking disapproving, I resign, so you will have to knead on the rug and stroke yourself. Well, obviously, Larry, this upset Ghost terribly: I was sorry as soon as I had said it. To try to make things a little bit better, I have agreed that we will not let Second Employee go for *a single moment unattended* until Ghost is sure she has regained a point of emotional stability.

To this end, Ghost covers the top two floors of the house, and has been supervising Second Employee doing something SILLY with sequins and 'sorting out all her running leggings', and I do the bottom two floors. For instance, last night I sat on the table MIAOWING while she was FAFFING in the kitchen before bed, and when she leaned over to fill the dishwasher I bit her on the bottom. Of course, it's a lot of trouble for me, but I'm just pleased to be contributing to familial harmony.

There is one thing which is worrying me slightly, Larry: I actually can't find Second Employee's employment contract after all that. I thought I remembered stapling it to the back of the Strategic Plan. But it doesn't seem to be there, and I've looked everywhere - under all the sofas, behind the back of First Employee's Pig Collection, inside the fridge, everywhere. In fact, Second Employee keeps picking me up and saying, what are you looking for, Mr Nosey. And I'm trying to do it discreetly! Larry, if you could just email me a copy of Second Employee's

Employment Contract before Ghost finds out I've lost it that would be wonderful (please don't copy Ghost in) - many thanks, and I will try ONCE AGAIN to be the firm anchor that keeps things in the High Peak on an even keel for at least another week!

October 2022

Larry and the Catinet, this is Ghost here, Ambassador to the High Peak, updating you on developments and despairing slightly about the calibre of Employees I am provided with. Today, instead of doing the ironing, Second Employee finished knitting a Small Silly Jumper of a kind which is too tiny for anyone, even a mole or one of the fairies who live at the bottom of the garden Disapproving of the Alliums. She said the electricity was off because there was a man downstairs updating the fusebox so she couldn't, but I am sure this was just an excuse (note to self: ask Esso to Google rechargeable irons to prove to Second Employee they exist. Surely they do!). I do not understand the purpose of the tiny non-functional jumper. Second Employee says she is going to give them to people for Christmas and 'they will think they are cute and they can hang them from the tree'. Larry, I foresee a diplomatic crisis approaching with rapidity. Can you imagine if some unsuspecting kind person hands Second Employee a proper Christmas present which has been bought in a shop and is competently manufactured, like, for example, a box of chocolates or a John Lewis voucher or something sensible and useful like that, and in return she gives them a miniature Woolly Jumper *with no use at all that I can see* and some Ridiculous Chutney? They will be furious. It will be all I can do, Larry, to keep things diplomatically on an even keel. I have asked Esso to mark out 23rd-28th December in our diaries, as these are the dates I think we are most at danger from the Diplomatic Incidents that will inevitably ensue.

Larry, you are more practiced than most at what to do when Employees set off on a Ridiculous Course Of Action that they cannot be dissuaded from: perhaps we can set up a Zoom for next Wednesday and you could share any tips? I must say, I do feel better knowing you have been through it too, and so recently as well!

Also, Esso isn't being helpful at all. He has been reading something Very Silly online in Feline HR Monthly about making your Employees feel valued, and I had some difficulty dissuading him from setting up Employee of The Week, which would have been a lot of trouble and which he would have only wanted to give to Second Employee anyway, because she is his favourite although no-one knows why, it is utterly incomprehensible, because say what you will about First Employee being loud and grabbing FEETIES but at least he is competent, or *at least we thought he was*!

Because, Esso discovered that it was Second Employee's birthday last week, and after a long discussion he persuaded me that it would be 'a nice gesture' to ask First Employee to get her a Birthday Card from us. Well, I knew it was going to go wrong as soon as we saw the envelope, which was addressed to Employee Number Two, and which made Esso think of Mambo Number Five, which he has been singing ever since. Then Second Employee opened the card up, and Esso and I looked at the front. It stated the following: 'Happy Birthday from your Pet'. Perhaps the most misguidedly poignant aspect of the whole affair is that First Employee has tried to correct it by making it refer to a plural, rather than a single, 'pet' - and has ignored the absolute, fundamental inappropriateness of the whole thing! Pet! Pet! Esso said, look Ghost, he's still learning, also it's probably from Aldi and they perhaps had limited choice. But Larry, when it is revealed that someone's entire conception of their job is this far removed from reality, what is there to do? Esso said, perhaps we can send him off to do Benchmarking. Benchmarking! Larry, when an Employee is this far gone, it is Beyond Benchmarking! The irony that all this time I have been worrying about Second Employee and her inadequacies, whereas she at least seems to understand our relationship: but First Employee has been going blithely on thinking he is having a lovely time, living with his 'pets'. Pets! Oh, I can't bear it. I must confess, Larry, that everything seems a little pointless at the moment. I have retreated to under the sofa, and I will grab Second Employee's ankle later to cheer myself up, but it will be a long time before I can get over the Pet slur. I may have to ask you to compel First Employee to make some kind of formal apology, Larry: I think that might help a bit. On the front page of the Times should do it. Yes, that might be the route to go down, actually, if you don't mind - I'll discuss formally with Esso and then get back to you!

November 2022

Larry, this is Esso here, Ambassador to the High Peak. Larry, I know you're a little busy at the moment, but I need your advice… I've tried so hard to defend Second Employee's aesthetic choices to Ghost, but now she's come home with an enormous crocheted spider called Boris which she says she found in the Cancer Research Shop in Buxton, and I think when Ghost discovers him it might all kick off… I wondered if you thought I should write an Emergency Interim Aesthetic Difference Resolution Policy, or just hide out on the spare room bed until things settle down? Many thanks for your advice! I do sometimes wish Ghost would be a little less rigid, but I know she'll look me straight in the eye and say Esso, what would Le Corbusier have said about having a crocheted spider in his machines for living, and I suppose I will see her point - Larry, it's all so difficult! I shall hope to be in touch soon in less fraught circumstances! Esso

November 2022

Larry and the Catinet. This is Esso, Ambassador to the High Peak, with an Important Observation. Larry, I wish you to imagine the following happy scene, which occurred earlier today on our sofa: Second Employee and I were doing her Daily Appraisal and Nuzzling. Imagine Second Employee smiling and relaxed, and not at all in terror of my Teeth, because she knows she is only likely to become very slightly PRESSED or SQUEEZED on the head by them when her hair is wet, when I accept that they do occasionally become slightly recalcitrant. I paint this picture for you, Larry, to illustrate my excellent, friendly and yet professional, relations with staff; and to demonstrate how unfair it is that Second Employee has managed to find YET MORE family members - how many family members has she got, Larry?! - to come and look at me and say, look, that is the fierce, scary cat who bit Paul.

In fact, Larry, it was even worse this time, because additional, rather wounding things were said, namely: a/ look at Esso looking a bit sinister, and b/ hello, Esso, did you enjoy Halloween. Larry, I think the remark about Halloween in particular was very hurtful, because you and I both know that it implies there is something slightly dark, or satanic about me, when this is not the case.

Second Employee tries to make things better, but she is not very good at it, because she does not have my Tact and Political Nous. She says, Esso isn't sinister, he is my special precious velvety friend (which I am), and he only looks a little bit like a demon because of his yellow eyes. How is that last bit helpful? I think it is very telling that Second Employee's one and only foray into PR many, many years ago ended in her causing trouble by using such an unflattering photograph of one of the History Professors for the University Newsletter that everyone thought she was doing it to be Subversive, which she was not; she was merely 'in a rush' and 'did not think to crop out his stomach'. Just like she 'didn't think' to blur the Under-eye Bags of the Then Vice Chancellor! As in much of her career, she was mainly focused on where the nearest cake shop was to her office rather than delivering her Objectives with Professionalism and Elegance! As you know, Larry, this is a continued moral failing which Ghost and I have tried almost constantly to correct, with, I am afraid to say, very mixed success.

Ghost says, actually why not just own it, Esso, there is nothing wrong with being a Small House Demon, it is a very dignified profession which runs in our family, because you and I both know about Granny on our Mother's Side who was half - well, Larry, actually, I don't think this is the time or place for discussing Granny on our Mother's Side, because Ghost and I have both come a very long way since then. We are

Professional Ambassadors, and we are not half or a fraction of anything, and there is nothing sinister about us at all; moreover, I shall reiterate very strongly that although Ghost *does* have her Familiar's Licence, she is *very definitely* currently non-practising; and we remain entirely focused on delivering the Feline Diplomatic Service High Peak Strategic Plan 2022-2023!

November 2022

Larry and the Catinet, this is Ghost, Joint Ambassador to the High Peak, with a COMPLAINT. Larry, Esso is being RIDICULOUS and I would like you to tell him to stop it, please. He'd been MAUNDERING about again because he had 'very gently touched Second Employee with his teeth and then closed them very slightly on her shoulder' to try to encourage her to play Chasey and at least get a bit of exercise rather than sitting about eating cake while reading books about cake: then he heard her asking First Employee 'if he thought it might be possible to stop Esso biting' and First Employee saying, ha ha definitely not, look at you over there Mr Bitey Esso.

Esso was upset because he says he does not want his nickname to be Mr Bitey Esso, even though I would like to point out, Larry, that I myself have the Utter Indignity of First Employee calling me Mrs G 'because she has an expression like an officious 1950s boarding house landlady': I merely rise above, and consider which of First Employee's shoes I may wish to pee in when the time comes. Anyway, Esso said he was doubly hurt because Second Employee knows they are Top Best Friends, and he isn't bitey: so I felt I had to give him a pep talk. I said, look Esso, you cannot get attached to Employees: Employees come and go, their brains are very tiny, and they are nothing but trouble anyway. What you should do, Esso, is think of yourself as a lone wolf, master of your own self, slicing like a blade through the darkness of our back lane; a pair of yellow eyes in the storm. Not sitting about purring and rubbing your cheek against Second Employee's, and rolling on your back with all your FEETIES in the air for anyone to grab. More John Wayne, Esso, less Richard Madeley: Andrew Tate is back on Twitter and you've got to re-embrace Toxic Masculinity. Go on, Esso, show Second Employee you don't need her! Larry, my only thought, as ever, was to make Esso more emotionally resistant: I had no other motive.

So Esso went off for a Dramatic Walk to be the Ernest Hemingway of Our Back Lane, and while he was gone, I thought I would be very kind and get Second Employee's daily appraisal done myself. First I took a selfie of us together, like Esso does, to show that he isn't the only one who thinks he has a good relationship with staff: and then Second Employee and I were sitting together, and I had taken her through her KPIs (she is doing very badly) and was getting some really productive PURRING and KNEADING done, when Esso came back. It turns out, Larry, that he had only managed to be Ernest

Hemingway down as far as Grey Next Door Cat's house, and Grey Next Door Cat had reminded him that actually he has eschewed toxic masculinity and is in touch with his emotions now, which was very unhelpful of Grey Next Door Cat in the circumstances.

Apparently Grey Next Door Cat had told him he'd got to 'hold the line', because now he is in touch with his emotions too, and he spends his time lounging about and purring which he likes much better. Anyway, Esso had processed this and run straight back into the house 'just to check Second Employee wasn't doing anything she needed his help with', and the first I knew of this was when I looked up from my KNEADING to find him staring at me with an expression of betrayal and fury, which I need hardly say to you, Larry, was quite inappropriate. Ghost, he said, you got rid of me on purpose so you could have Second Employee all to yourself! Well, Larry, of course this is nonsense. I would never, ever do such a thing, and if Second Employee thinks I am the softest and the prettiest cat in the whole of the High Peak and very possibly the wider Stockport area, well, that is only because I am. But, because of this, Esso has broken our code, and he is visiting Second Employee when she does Unhelpful Things With Wool And Fabric on the top floor, and Lounging on the Employees' Bed which he KNOWS is reserved for me!

Larry, this is a critical time of the year: soon Second Employee will be making her Christmas preparations, and without very, very strict supervision from me, who knows what will happen. She could well emerge from her room on the top floor with a life-size replica of Santa made from pompoms, or WORSE. I've already noticed a Colin The Caterpillar tree decoration LURKING about from when she was given a Marks and Spencer voucher by someone who clearly expected her to spend it on something sensible, like beige pants! Larry, please tell Esso to stay in the basement like he's supposed to, to leave Second Employee alone, and to stop having emotional needs because all they do is cause trouble!

November 2022

Larry, this is Esso, Ambassador to the High Peak, with a Staffing Update. Larry, Second Employee has had a Silly Concern, and I am proud to say that because of the *hours* I have put into maintaining excellent feline-Employee relations, she chose to come to me to help her with it. I was lounging on the back of the Downstairs Sofa with my back pressed against the radiator, and she came to sit on the sofa with me, which I like, because then I can press against her with my Feeties and Purr. I could tell she was thinking about something, so I purred to assure her that I am always here to listen, obviously unless I'm eating, or engaged in a particularly engrossing game of Chasey, or having to intimidate Hairy Black Cat who keeps walking up our back lane and looking at me in a way I'm interpreting as Unhelpfully Territorial, or chasing a ball of wool round the table leg. But at all other times.

Anyway. Second Employee said, Esso. We're coming up to the festive season, and you know what that means, lots of visitors, some of them older and not in great health, and also you know First Employee and I go down South for a couple of nights to see family. Well, while we're gone, my mum and dad might come and look after you. Now, Esso, you know dad hasn't been too well and mum is a bit nervous of cats, so, one of the things which is really, really not going to help family relationships is if anyone, especially dad, manages to get bitten by anyone's teeth again, especially at Christmas. Do you and I understand each other, Esso? Well, Larry, of course I understood! I was proud that Second Employee had chosen to come to me with her Minor Employee Worries. I reassured her by butting her with my head, and of course I took swift, practical action. Later that evening, I went to Ghost and said, Ghost, Second Employee is worried you're going to bite her father at Christmas, so *you'd better make sure you don't*.

Well, Larry, Ghost hasn't had my training in Employee Relations, and she gave me *such a look*, and said, what did Second Employee say exactly, Esso. So I told her, word for word, because of my excellent memory and cognitive skills which I hone every day by playing Wordle with Grey Next Door

Cat, and she said - and you won't believe this, Larry - she said, honestly Esso, sometimes I worry you believe your own hype. Probably next week you'll come and tell me you're actually Napoleon or Julius Caesar and I shall say to you the same as I'm going to say to you now: Esso, listen to yourself, I can see right through you. Larry! Can you believe Ghost could be so rude to me? Although she certainly can be quite a rude cat - I think we can both remember what she said when she found out Matt Hancock was going to be in I'm A Celebrity. It really is a shame, because if she was less rude, perhaps Second Employee would come to her with her troubles, just like she does to me. But never mind - I have to pick my battles, and I cannot make my sister a better, more civil Feline. I must take her as she is. It's a hard road, Larry, the Moral High Road, but I console myself with the knowledge that whatever else is happening I, at least, am doing my Duty!

Chapter 8

December 2022: the fight to keep Christmas Aesthetic

December 2022

Larry and the Catinet. This is Ghost, Ambassador to the High Peak, with my Very Helpful Update. Larry, I have a number of things to appraise you of. Firstly, something we were expecting has not happened, but something we were NOT expecting has. Last year at almost exactly this time, Second Employee became OBSESSED with the creation of a Christmas Pudding, which involved folding greaseproof paper, boiling basins full of what appeared, frankly, to be mostly nutmeg for nine hours, and levels of stress hitherto reserved for UN Peacekeeping Missions. Esso and I made a note in the High Peak Strategic Diary at the time, and so, when the time of year rolled around again, we were POISED and READY: but, Larry, this will astonish you. She just said, oh what does it all matter when everything is terrible anyway (which is an Unhelpful Attitude which we will be discussing with her in her next appraisal), and produced a very strange chocolate and fig concoction which we are sure she will regret.

We thought we had got away lightly: but then First Employee, entirely unexpectedly, became EQUALLY UNHELPFULLY

OBSESSED with something called Panettone, and it turns out that Second Employee also has very strong feelings about Panettone, but on the other side! The Employees are divided! Second Employee says her feelings about Panettone were summed up in 2013 in a Guardian article by Julie Bindel, and she 'agrees with every word that woman has said about Panettones even though she doesn't entirely see eye to eye with her with regards to the actual widespread practical application of Radical Feminist Lesbian Separatism'. Larry, I do not know the details of Second Employee's views on the actual practicalities of Radical Feminist Lesbian Separatism, but I hope they are anti; because we haven't got time for her to be doing anything radical at all. Especially since she told Esso she might recommit to learning Sanskrit in 2023, and we're worried enough about how that's going to impact on her already very inadequate delivery of the workplan!

Anyway, First Employee says he wants a Christmas Panettone, and he is going to make one in the breadmaker and that will show everyone, especially Second Employee. I can reassure you, Larry, that Esso and I are taking very decisive action to counter this small difficulty. Esso began by going Down Our Back Lane to ask Grey Next Door Cat what a Panettone actually is, and, reassuringly, it's some kind of Italian Brioche With Mixed Peel, so we don't believe they're illegal. So we have decided to let First Employee get on with it, and at the very worst, Second Employee will just have to eat a lot of Mixed Peel Toast.

Secondly, I have been supervising very, very carefully the small woollen figurines which Second Employee has placed on the Ikea sideboard in the sitting room. Unfortunately, earlier, I turned to make a closer examination of the standard of seaming on the woolly sheep figurine in particular, and somehow I missed my footing and fell off the sideboard, taking the rest of the Tableau with me. Second Employee was ineffectual: she descended on me squawking, Ghost, you have Decimated the Baby Jesus and the entire Holy Family, what are you doing. I have, of course, updated the Risk Register accordingly, but, Larry, could we notify all Employees that all silly Woollen Idols must be placed so as to cause no inconvenience to Feline Employers. Many thanks.

Thirdly, and most importantly, Esso told me that, the other day when Second Employee's Parents were Drinking Coffee in our Downstairs again, he popped down to say hello to Second Employee's Mother: because Esso is still trying to do Diplomatic Work after the Bite, but honestly, Larry, as you will see, his efforts are wasted. Esso's appearance provoked an Unhelpful Train Of Thought in Second Employee's Mother, which ended in her stating that Second Employee's Family are all Dog People and that, for at least five generations, Second Employee is the only one who has ever 'had cats'. Larry, leaving aside the Utter Unsuitability of this particular Possessive Verb, I have thought about this very carefully, and I would like you to ban Second Employee's Mother from the house. I do not think she is a good influence. I do not want these kind of thoughts circulating. I would like to remind you, Larry, that although I am *currently* (of course, in absence of correctly-completed paperwork) non-practicing, I was top of the class in my Familiar Exams, and I could cause a lot of trouble if I was unhappy. Really a *great deal of trouble*. I look forward to hearing you have communicated the Ban effectively! Many thanks, Larry, and I shall update again soon!

(Larry, this is Esso - I'm really sorry. I'll talk to Ghost yet again about it *not being appropriate to make threats to people*. Please be assured I'll ensure she continues to be non-practicing! I've got her completely under control!)

December 2022

Larry and the Catinet. This is Ghost again, Ambassador to the High Peak, with news of a Christmas Miracle! Larry, something *wonderful* has happened - First Employee has had to have a Really Painful Operation! Esso said to me, Ghost, be careful you don't come across as a tiny bit callous, but Larry, it's honestly nothing major; just something to do with his Carpal Tunnel whatever that is - I *personally* think it's something that *primarily* goes wrong on Employees who are Morally Weak -

and now he has a big bandage on his hand. And this means, Larry, that he can't drive, so the Employees aren't going to leave us and go Down South, because Second Employee is rubbish at driving long distances, especially since her brother got stuck for eight hours on the M6 coming back from the Lake District and she took it personally. In fact she says it tested her to the limit having to drive First Employee back from Macclesfield General Hospital over the Cat and Fiddle, which is a road Second Employee is very frightened of, solely for the Very Silly and Self-Indulgent Reason that it is statistically the most deadly road in England, or some such nonsense.

But at least it means Second Employee won't now suddenly take it into her head to go driving on the M3! So we won't have to be looked after by Second Employee's Parents, and that means I won't have to spend the two days Constantly Monitoring what Esso's teeth are doing and with what - or with *whom* - they might be in contact! Finally, Larry, I feel I can rest. And, as a Wonderful Christmas Bonus, while Second Employee was waiting for First Employee, she went to look round a large shop called Arighi Bianchi, which has furniture in. Well, Larry, only Second Employee could find a shop called something so SILLY: if I had a furniture shop, for example, I would call it Ghost's Furniture Shop, and that would be much better: but, Second Employee said she walked round being slightly overwhelmed by all the grey things and marble tables, and wondered 'whether she should have gone for a more minimalist look' in the Embassy. Larry, I hear Choirs of Christmas Angels Sing. Perhaps FINALLY Second Employee has seen the light. Perhaps the UTTER RIDICULOUSNESS that is her rainbow tree downstairs has tipped her over the edge, and she will buy a giant tin of Ammonite paint which has been colour matched to a cheaper base and set to work on 1st January. In fact I think this will definitely happen, although, as Esso says, she did spend about twenty minutes earlier trying to hang a glittery blue bauble from my tail, which does not *entirely* bode well for her being a Better and More Sensible Employee.

There are only two things which concern us now, Larry. Firstly, we were initially a bit worried that now First Employee has had his Carpal Tunnel sorted out, he might start playing the Cello, which is Lurking at the back of the sitting room. We thought about this, though, and Esso says he thinks the problem with First Employee and the Cello is not that his Carpal Tunnel was stopping him playing it but that he spent the time in his Youth when he should have been practicing it drinking cocktails made of Vodka and Barley Wine, arguing with people about Gramsci, and experimenting not entirely successfully with Polyamory. So that is reassuring, because Second Employee and I both agree that First Employee needs to carry on with his practising of the Piano, and not get distracted: perhaps one day he will be good enough to play the Ballad of Barry and Freda, and not just Bach! Secondly, though - and this is a real concern - now First Employee will not be able to move his hand much for a fortnight, Second Employee is going to have to cook Christmas Dinner. Larry, this is very, very serious: First Employee always cooks the ENTIRE Christmas Dinner while Second Employee merely FAFFS about arranging candles, 'entertaining' her family, and trying to work out what you do with a charger plate and failing. She has not realised the enormity of the situation yet, Larry: but Esso and I are already picturing her trying to get the Pigs In Blankets ready at the same time as the Stuffing, with First Employee HOVERING and disapproving of gravy granules and Second Employee's Mother having an OPINION on the roast potatoes. Larry, I fear there will be a meltdown. I fear it is inevitable. All Esso and I can do, I feel, is to rest as much as possible, and try to face what will be a Very Trying Weekend with as much equanimity as is possible in the circumstances!

December 2022

Larry and the Catinet; this is Esso, Ambassador to the High Peak, wishing you and your Employees a Happy and Productive New Year. Ghost and I would also like to extend our good wishes, just this once, to those Employees who we know occasionally read these updates without Explicit Catinet Permission. Even Reluctant Potential Employees who set bad examples. Perhaps they might all be inspired to become Better Employees in 2023. We certainly hope Second Employee will: she has not, I'm afraid, Larry, distinguished herself over the Christmas period. In fact there was an incident involving a

Kazoo which we won't discuss. Luckily she did get some Paperwhites to bloom on time (although she's still no Sarah Raven!), and that went in her favour somewhat. Even so, Ghost has had to be very firm with her appraisal! Anyway Happy New Year to everyone, and let this be the year we finally all deliver on our Strategic Plans!

[Note from Esso: we ended 2022 on a happy, relatively innocent note. The next couple of years were to be rather a test of my diplomacy. For example, I was directly accused of murder: Ghost attempted to create a militia and invade South Yorkshire: First Employee revealed a love of madrigals. But we will leave all that for the next volume. Imagine us, all happy together, as we were then: the Employees lounging on the sofas, me lounging on my throw, Ghost lounging under the tree and threatening with a deft paw the integrity of the 1950s Glass Decorations Second Employee had bought from eBay: replete with biscuits, chocolate, coffee and Good Cheer, and ready to take on all the challenges to come!]

THE END

About The Author

Susie lives with her husband in a very tall house in the High Peak in Derbyshire, where the winters are long and the cats are feisty. She has a great many uncool hobbies and tries never to leave the house, but has hitherto been unsuccessful in this endeavour.

She has a substack at susie.halksworth.substack.com

Printed in Dunstable, United Kingdom